Hollyhock And Sticky Buns

NETTLES B&B PARA COZY
BOOK ONE

CHRISSY CHICORY

HALF-PAST 2 PUBLISHING

ISBN (Print - Amazon): 978-1-963402-15-5

ISBN (Print - Draft2Digital): 978-1-963402-17-9

LCCN 2025905053

Published by Half-Past 2 Publishing

Edited by Kimberly Huther

 Formatted with Vellum

For Nana Teresa—whose baking outshines even Nan Nettles—may your kitchen always be filled with warmth, laughter, and the most delicious treats.

Contents

Hollyhock and Sticky Buns

Chrissy Chicory

The Hurricane's Gift

The storm raged like a restless beast, its howls battering the Mossy Mobile with gusts that rattled the windows. Rain lashed the windshield in furious sheets, transforming the world beyond into a kaleidoscope of distorted shadows.

Inside, Nan Nettles clutched the dashboard with one hand and adjusted her rain-spattered flamingo-print dress with the other.

"Mossy, do try to keep us on the road," she implored. "This gale feels like the tempest from *The Tempest*, but I'd rather not have us washed ashore like Prospero and company."

"Fear not, my muse. The great Bard himself couldn't have orchestrated a more thrilling scene for us!" Mossy proclaimed.

The wipers struggled to clear the deluge as Mossy maneuvered the RV through winding Florida backroads. Outside, lightning cracked, illuminating dense oaks shrouded in Spanish moss. The GPS had given up miles ago, and Nan had decided to follow the one thing she trusted more than modern technology—her gut.

"There!" she cried, pointing through the rain. "I think I

saw a light! Perhaps a reflection off a window? Mossy, head that way."

The RV sputtered and coughed, lurching forward one last time before coming to a halt in the overgrown front yard of the abandoned home. Mossy furrowed his brow as he tried the ignition, to no avail.

"I'm afraid our trusty steed has given up the ghost, my dear," he said.

Nan blinked with expectancy. "Well then, we simply must seek refuge in this charming abode! Oh, Mossy, can't you just imagine the stories these walls could tell?"

Mossy hesitated, his practical nature warring with his wife's infectious enthusiasm. "Nan, my love, I'm not certain that's entirely wise. This house looks as though it hasn't seen a living soul in decades."

"Precisely!" Nan exclaimed, already unbuckling her seat-belt. "All the more reason to explore! Who knows what delightful mysteries await us within?"

As Mossy opened his mouth to protest further a particularly loud crack of thunder shook the RV, making his decision for him.

"Very well," he acquiesced, a hint of amusement in his voice. "Lead on, my intrepid adventurer. But do try to remember, darling, that not every creak and groan is a ghostly manifestation."

The silhouette of the grand Victorian house loomed ahead, its spires piercing the storm-torn sky like ghostly sentinels. Lightning illuminated its peeling paint and ivy-choked walls, casting fleeting shadows that danced like specters in the night.

The windows glowed faintly with reflections of the flashing heavens above, a beacon in the chaos.

The storm roared on, but here in the shadow of the house there was a strange stillness.

"Nan," Mossy began, peering up at the structure, "I hate to play Cassandra, but this place looks as though it could collapse at any moment."

"Rubbish!" Nan declared, adjusting her hat now dripping with rain. "It's splendid. Like a story waiting to be written." She paused, a rare moment of vulnerability flickering across her face. "Don't you feel it, Mossy? Like we were meant to find this place—a fresh chapter for us."

Mossy lingered on the threshold, the flashlight cumbersome in his hand. "Nan, do you ever wonder if your boundless enthusiasm might lead us astray?" She turned, her brown and gray curls soaked flat by the rain, and grinned. "Only into the most marvelous of adventures, darling. Now hurry, or you'll miss it!"

The porch creaked beneath their feet, a sound too human in its protest. As they neared the towering double doors, a faint, sweet scent—lavender, perhaps—rose from the wood, incongruous with the storm-drenched air. Nan ran her fingers over the intricate carvings on the brass handle—a swirling motif of roses and ivy. It was oddly warm, despite the chill of the storm.

"How odd," Mossy said, "Look there. The key has been left in the lock!"

Nan smiled as she turned the antique skeleton key. As if answering her touch, the door groaned open. She stepped inside, her heels tapping sharply against the cracked marble floor. The air carried an odd welcome, thick with the scent of aged wood, mildew and, inexplicably, lavender.

The faint floral aroma seemed to linger just at the edge of perception, teasing her senses. Lightning flared, illuminating the grand staircase that swept upward like the spine of a forgotten story.

"It's perfect," she whispered, her voice reverent. Her fingers traced the banister, her touch lingering as though she could coax its secrets to life.

Mossy lingered on the threshold, his flashlight carving jagged beams through the dimness. The light glanced off a tarnished chandelier, its crystals swaying gently despite the still air, as though touched by an unseen hand. "Perfectly eerie," he quipped, though his gaze softened as he watched Nan, her curls glowing like a halo in the dim light.

Ever the pragmatist, Mossy shined his flashlight into the gloom. "It certainly has personality," he said, glancing at Nan. "Are you certain we're alone?"

Before Nan could respond, a low creak echoed through the house. She froze, her hand tightening around the key. In the distance, she thought she saw movement—a flicker of white disappearing up the staircase.

"Did you see that?" she whispered.

Mossy followed her gaze, his brow furrowed. "See what, my dear?"

Nan hesitated. The storm outside seemed impossibly distant now, muffled by the house's thick walls. She shook her head. "Probably just my imagination."

But as they moved deeper into the house, she couldn't shake the feeling that they were being watched. Not by anything sinister, but something... curious.

Nan stepped into the dimly lit foyer, her sandals leaving a trail of tiny puddles on the dusty marble floor. The air was thick with the scent of aged wood and forgotten memories.

A bolt of lightning lit up the grand staircase, creating eerie silhouettes that seemed to dance across the peeling wallpaper. For a brief moment, she thought she saw the figure of a woman amongst the shadows. However, when she turned back for another look, there was nothing there. Just a mere trick of the light.

"Mossy, darling," Nan breathed, her eyes sparkling with excitement, "can you imagine what this place must have been like in its heyday? Oh, the parties, the scandals... the secrets!"

Mossy followed, his gaze drawn to a cobweb-draped chandelier. "I daresay, Nan, it does have a certain charm."

Nan paused, a mischievous glint in her eye. "Now, let's see if we can't bring some light to this gloomy old place." As if on cue, she spotted a collection of candles on a nearby side table. With nimble fingers, she began arranging them around the room. "Mossy, be a dear and see if you can't get a fire going in that marvelous fireplace," she called over her shoulder. "I have the most wonderful idea brewing."

Mossy raised an eyebrow but obliged, kneeling before the hearth. "And what grand scheme are you concocting now, my love?"

Nan twirled, her sundress billowing around her. "Can't you see it, Mossy? This isn't just a house—it's our future! A bed and breakfast, filled with charm, mystery, and just a touch of the supernatural. We'll be the talk of Daytona Beach!"

As Mossy coaxed the fire to life, he was swept up in Nan's enthusiasm. "I must admit the idea does have a certain appeal. Though I shudder to think what our granddaughters would say about us embarking on such an adventure at our age. They do so like to visit us in the Keys. Our tiny condo is easy to maintain. This—" he opined as he gazed around the room, "— would be quite the undertaking."

Nan's eyes twinkled in the growing firelight. "Oh, pish posh. Age is but a number, and we've got plenty of life left in us yet." Her eyes gleamed with unbridled excitement as she ran her fingers along the ornate wainscoting, disturbing years of settled dust.

Mossy, caught up in his wife's infectious enthusiasm, found himself nodding. "Indeed, my dear. It would be quite a challenge to bring her back to the splendor of yesteryear."

"Precisely!" Nan exclaimed, clapping her hands. "We simply must uncover the history of this grand old dame. I can feel it in my bones—there's something special here, something... otherworldly."

Mossy chuckled, adjusting his spectacles. "Now, now, let's not get carried away with fanciful notions of the supernatural."

"Darling," Nan said, fixing him with a look of fond exasperation, "where's your sense of romance? Of mystery?"

Before Mossy could respond, a flash of lightning illuminated a door at the end of the hall. "The library!" they exclaimed in unison.

"Good heavens," Mossy whispered, drinking in the sight of floor-to-ceiling bookshelves, leather-bound tomes, and a massive mahogany desk.

Nan grinned mischievously. "What was that about fanciful notions, dear?"

Mossy, already perusing the shelves, waved a hand distractedly. "I stand corrected, my love. This... this is beyond my wildest dreams."

His eyes fell upon a crystal decanter. "Is that...?" He uncorked it, inhaling deeply. "By Jove, it is! Thirty-year-old Scotch, if I'm not mistaken."

"Well then," Nan said, procuring two glasses from a nearby cabinet, "it would be a shame to let it go to waste, wouldn't it?"

As Mossy poured, Nan considered. "It's as if the house knew exactly what we needed."

"To new beginnings," Mossy toasted, raising his glass.

"And old spirits," Nan added with a wink.

Nan gazed around the room, her mind racing with possibilities. "Mossy, darling, can't you just see it? This library filled with guests sipping tea and sharing ghost stories by the fire?"

Mossy looked up from his Tennyson, a smile of amusement playing on his lips. "I'm not sure our future patrons would appreciate being scared out of their wits, my dear."

"Oh, pish posh," Nan spouted, waving her hand dismissively. "A little fright is good for the constitution. Besides, we'll balance it out with your poetry readings and my famous scones."

She twirled around the room, her sundress billowing like a Victorian lady's skirts. "We'll call it 'Nettles B&B: Where Every Stay is a Spirited Adventure!'"

Mossy chuckled, shaking his head fondly. "You're positively glowing, Nan. I haven't seen you this excited since you found that 'haunted' rolling pin at the flea market."

"That rolling pin was haunted, I tell you," Nan retorted, wagging her finger. "How else do you explain those perfectly even pie crusts?"

Their laughter was interrupted by a sharp knock at the front door. Nan froze, exchanging a worried glance with Mossy.

"Good heavens," she whispered, "who could that be in this weather?"

As if on cue they realized the storm had calmed, replaced by an eerie stillness. Mossy set down his book and glass, rising to answer the door.

"Wait," Nan hissed, grabbing his arm. "What if it's... you know... not of this world?"

Mossy patted her hand reassuringly. "My dear, I doubt spectral beings would bother with knocking."

They made their way to the entrance hall, Nan clutching Mossy's arm. As he opened the door they found themselves face to face with two police officers, their uniforms damp from the recent downpour.

"Good evening," the taller officer said, one eyebrow raised quizzically. "We received reports of a break-in at this address. Mind explaining what you're doing here?"

Nan's face broke into a radiant smile, her theatrical nature taking center stage. "Why, Officer, you're looking at the new owners of this magnificent establishment!"

The officers exchanged skeptical glances as Mossy cleared his throat nervously. "What my wife means to say is—"

"We've only just acquired the property," Nan interrupted smoothly. "We simply need to get in touch with the real estate agent to finalize the paperwork. Isn't that right, darling?"

Mossy nodded weakly, marveling at Nan's ability to spin stories on the spot. He could almost see the gears turning in her head, weaving their unexpected adventure into the fabric of her imagined B&B empire.

The officers still looked unconvinced, but Nan was in her element now. "Why don't you come in for a cup of tea? I'm sure we can sort this all out like civilized folk. And who knows? You might be our very first guests!"

As Nan ushered the bemused officers into the entrance hall, Mossy's attention drifted back to the leather-bound Tennyson. The poetry called to him like a siren's song, and he found himself sauntering back to the library and sinking into the depths of the armchair, lost in the lyrical verses.

"You see, Officers," Nan's voice lilted through the air, her hands gesticulating wildly, "this house simply spoke to us. It was as if the very walls whispered, 'Nan and Mossy Nettles, welcome home!'"

The younger officer scratched his head, clearly overwhelmed by Nan's effervescent charm. "Ma'am, I'm not sure that's how property acquisition works..."

"Oh, but it is!" Nan insisted. "In matters of the heart and hearth, one must trust in the whispers of fate. Isn't that right, Mossy dear?"

Mossy, engrossed in a particularly moving stanza, merely hummed in agreement, his fingers tracing the gilt edges of the pages.

Nan's gaze softened as she glanced at her husband, a fond smile playing on her lips. "You'll have to excuse him, Officers. When Mossy finds a kindred spirit in literature, the world around him simply fades away."

The older officer cleared his throat. "Be that as it may, we still need to see some form of documentation..."

"Of course, of course." Nan nodded sagely, her mind whirring with possibilities. "I'm sure we can locate the papers in one of these charming antique desks. Why, I wouldn't be surprised if we found a century-old deed hidden away in a secret compartment!"

"Ma'am, that's not what we meant," the tall officer stated.

Nan led the increasingly bewildered officers on a whimsical tour of the house. As they reached the parlor, a chill brushed her cheek and the faintest whisper tickled her ear. "Welcome," it seemed to say. She paused, her heart quickening, before turning back to her bemused guests with a radiant smile.

This house with its creaking floorboards and whispered secrets was destined to become their home. Their very own Nettles Bed and Breakfast.

Standing in the entrance hall, Nan gazed fondly at Mossy, his figure bathed in the golden glow of firelight. A soft creak drew her attention upward. At the top of the grand staircase, a shadow shifted—too large to be imagined and too silent to be mundane. Her breath caught, but when she blinked it was gone. Only the lingering scent of lavender remained, sweet and unsettling. The storm outside had calmed, leaving behind a peculiar stillness. A gentle breeze wafted through an open window, carrying with it the scent of rain-soaked earth and possibility.

"Isn't it strange," she murmured, more to herself than anyone else, "the way the wind blows?"

A Victorian Welcome

~~~

The ancient quill pen scratched across parchment, its feather trembling with each stroke as if alive. Nan beamed as she signed the final flourish on the deed. The kitchen of the dilapidated Victorian manor creaked and groaned around them, as if the very house held its breath.

"There we are, Mrs. Hawthorne." Nan slid the papers across the table, and to her surprise they flew through the air like leaves in a gust of wind. They landed on the floor, scattered around the room.

"My, my," Mossy exclaimed as he felt the wind, "it's quite breezy in here."

The real-estate agent frowned. "The windows are closed. I don't see where that came from."

The morning sun illuminated Nan's perfectly manicured nails, casting a pale iridescent-pink sheen over them as she gathered the papers into a haphazard pile. With each movement of her hand, the princess cut diamond on her white gold wedding ring caught the light and created dazzling prisms that danced around the room.

"It's only natural for old homes to have drafts," she

explained, smiling. "I do believe that makes us the proud new owners of this magnificent old girl." She carefully removed a tiny speck of lint from her white cashmere cardigan which was gracefully draped over her slender shoulders, adding a touch of softness to her vibrant yellow wrap dress.

The real estate agent's eyes darted nervously about the room as she gathered the documents into a folder and placed it in her brown-checked Reversible Neverfull.

"Oops, this paper isn't included in the contract," she said as she handed Nan a drawing.

"Thank you, dear. I was brainstorming ideas for a book earlier this morning."

"Nan is actually an incredible writer," Mossy chimed in.

"I must say, Mrs. Nettles, you two are full of surprises, aren't you?" The agent brushed her hands down her navy pantsuit. "I've never had a sale quite like this. The police calling to inform me of new buyers? Most unusual."

"Oh, don't be modest, Mrs. Hawthorne. I'm sure you have some interesting stories to share about your real estate business. You must come across all kinds of people and fantastical locations," Nan proclaimed.

Mrs. Hawthorne pursed her ruby lips as she tucked a strand of hair behind her ear, reveling a demure silver hoop earring. "It's not just unusual, Mrs. Nettles. It's... well, it's downright eerie. This house, you see, it's known to be... haunted."

Mossy, who had been observing the exchange, raised an eyebrow behind his spectacles. His gaze met Nan's, a silent conversation passing between them ending with matching smiles.

"Haunted, you say?" Nan leaned forward, her voice dropping to a conspiratorial whisper. "Do tell, Mrs. Hawthorne. Are we to expect rattling chains and moaning specters? Perhaps a headless horseman or two?"

Mrs. Hawthorne's face paled. "This is no laughing matter, Mrs. Nettles. The locals are terrified. Some won't even drive by the place. It's said that... that things happen here. Unnatural things."

Nan's smile never faltered, though her eyes softened with genuine warmth. "My dear Mrs. Hawthorne, I assure you we're quite prepared for any otherworldly tenants. Why, I'd say this grand old dame is simply crying out for a bit of love and attention."

As she spoke Nan's gaze drifted to the cracked stained-glass windows, where dust motes danced in shafts of golden sunlight. In her mind's eye she could already see the faded grandeur restored, the rooms filled with laughter and the clinking of teacups.

"Besides," she added with a wink, "what's a proper English tea without a ghost or two to liven things up?"

Mossy chuckled softly, his hair falling into his eyes as he shook his head. "My dear," he said, his voice rich with affection, "I do believe you'd invite the spirits themselves for scones and jam if given half the chance."

Nan reached across the table and trailed her fingers along the smooth, pressed sleeve of his crisp white button-up shirt. "And why not, darling? I'm sure they'd be delightful company. Much more interesting than some of the living guests we've entertained over the years."

Mrs. Hawthorne looked between the couple, her expression a mix of bewilderment and grudging admiration. "Well," she said, gathering her bag, "I can't say I understand it, but I wish you both the best of luck. You'll need it in this place."

"Mrs. Hawthorne," Nan said warmly, her voice carrying a hint of theatrical flair, "we simply cannot thank you enough for your assistance in acquiring this marvelous abode. I assure you, we shall nurture it as if it were our own dear child."

The real estate agent hurried towards the grand entrance,

her eyes nervously darting about as if expecting a spectral apparition to materialize at any moment. Her lips twitched in a reluctant smile as she replied, "Well, Mrs. Nettles, I do hope you know what you're getting in to. This house has quite the reputation."

Nan let out a hardy laugh. "Oh, my dear, the best houses always do. Why, I'd be terribly disappointed if it didn't come with at least one resident poltergeist!"

Mossy called after her, "Do come back for tea once we're settled, Mrs. Hawthorne!"

Nan proclaimed, "We'll save you a seat at the séance table!"

As Mrs. Hawthorne hurried down the overgrown path, Nan closed the hulking oak door with a satisfying thud. She leaned against it, her heart racing with excitement.

Her smile softened as she turned to her husband. "Well, my love," she said, "it seems we've embarked on quite the adventure."

Mossy nodded. "We have, my dear. Indeed, we have." He held out his hand, a long silver chain gleaming in the sunlight. Attached was the ornate skeleton key to the house. "For you." Mossy draped the necklace about her neck. "I've checked: the key opens not only the front door, but every door in the house."

"Oh, Mossy." Nan's voice trembled as she held back tears of joy.

Mossy kissed the top of her head. "I'm glad you are happy, Mrs. Nettles."

Nan's gaze swept across the dusty foyer. "Well, our darling new home," she whispered, "it seems it's just the three of us now."

* * *

Nan's footsteps echoed through the empty halls as she wandered deeper into the house. The air was thick with the scent of neglect and faded memories. Shafts of afternoon sunlight pierced through cracks in the boarded windows, illuminating motes of dust that danced like fairy lights.

Her eyes were drawn to a magnificent stained-glass window at the end of the corridor. Its vibrant hues were muted by a fine layer of grime, but the intricate design of intertwining roses was still breathtaking. A jagged crack ran through one pane, casting a prismatic rainbow across the faded wallpaper.

"Oh, you poor dear," Nan murmured, running her fingers along the peeling edges. The delicate pattern reminded her of antique lace, unraveling with the passage of time. "We'll have you looking splendid again in no time at all."

As she spoke a cool breeze whispered through the hall, carrying with it the faintest hint of jasmine. Nan's breath caught in her throat.

"Is that you, dear house?" she asked, her voice barely above a whisper. "Are you welcoming me home?"

Nan's heart fluttered with excitement as she pushed open a cumbersome oak door, revealing a dimly lit room. Dust motes swirled in the air, illuminated by a thin beam of light coming through a gap in the curtains. As her eyes adjusted to the gloom, Nan gasped.

There, by the window, stood a figure of ethereal beauty—a woman in an intricately detailed Victorian dress, her form shimmering at the edges like a mirage. Nan blinked, certain her eyes were playing tricks on her, but the apparition remained.

"Oh my," Nan breathed, her hand fluttering to the strand of pearls that graced her neck. "You're absolutely exquisite, aren't you?"

The ghost turned, fixing Nan with sharp eyes. Nan felt a thrill of excitement.

"I do hope I'm not interrupting anything," Nan ventured, her natural ebullience winning out over her momentary shock. "I'm Nan Nettles, your new roommate, as it were. Pleased to make your acquaintance."

For a moment, only silence answered her. Then, as if from a great distance, a voice reached Nan's ears. It was refined, tinged with an antiquated lilt that spoke of bygone days.

"Bithia," the ghost replied, a hint of curiosity dancing in her spectral eyes. Her head tilted slightly to the right. "You're handling this quite calmly for someone who has just come face to face with a spirit." She glided closer toward Nan. "I've seen all kinds of responses to such encounters, and most people don't react as well as you are. People think they want to see a ghost, but when the encounter actually happens it often proves overwhelming."

Nan laughed, a warm, inviting sound that seemed to chase away some of the room's gloom. "My dear Bithia, I find it all together wonderful! It's fabulous to meet you! Though I must admit I didn't expect it to happen quite so soon after moving in."

Bithia fixed her gaze on the key that hung from Nan's neck, resting near her heart.

Nan cautiously moved forward, her curiosity piqued. "I'm dying to learn more about you and why you've ended up in this particular location—this house." Nan surveyed the room, sensing its solemn energy. But she was dead set on changing that mood into one of elation. "This is so exhilarating!"

Bithia's spectral form shimmered, a playful smirk gracing her ethereal features. "My dear Nan, you've barely unpacked and already you're delving into the mysteries of the beyond. I admire your spirit." She paused, casting a mischievous glance around the room. "This was my childhood home. When I was alive, I could speak to the other side; I was what was known as a spiritualist. I held seances right in the parlor below." Her eyes showed a hint of longing.

Nan swept her gaze over Bithia's transparent form. She wore a tightly cinched corset, accentuating her hourglass figure, and her skirt was adorned with intricate embroidery and trim that obscured the layers of petticoats beneath. "You must have lived during the Victorian Era. Spiritualism was sweeping not only Europe, but America as well!" Nan exclaimed enthusiastically.

With a graceful wave of her translucent hand, Bithia approached an ornate Victorian table near the window. Nan watched, transfixed, as a series of sharp, staccato knocks emanated from the wooden surface.

"Table-rapping," Nan whispered, her voice filled with awe. "Just like in Grandmother's stories!"

Bithia's smile widened. "Oh, but we're just getting started, my dear. I was the talk of the town, their most interesting darling. All of the most important people from Upstate New York vacationed here when Flaggler and Rockefeller put it on the map."

To Nan's astonishment the table began to rise, hovering several inches above the faded carpet. She clapped in delight, feeling for all the world like a child at a magic show.

"Gracious me! And here I thought levitation was reserved for stage magicians," Nan exclaimed, her mind racing.

"Ah, the great Houdini himself tested me; he was quite skeptical. And even Sir Arthur Conan Doyle and his wife stayed in this very room during their visit." As if in a confirmation, a strange, misty substance began to form around Bithia's spectral form. It writhed and twisted, taking on impossible shapes before dissipating into the air.

"Ectoplasm," Nan breathed, her eyes wide with wonder. "I've read about it, but to see it with my own eyes..."

Bithia's voice carried a hint of pride. "It seems you're quite well-versed in the spiritualist arts, Nan. I daresay we'll get along splendidly."

Nan's heart swelled with excitement. What other secrets did this house hold? And how would her life change now that she shared her home with a Victorian ghost? "It must be so fun being a ghost."

Bithia considered. "I must say I enjoyed being the spiritualist that summoned the spirits more than being the spirit itself." Her spectral form dimmed slightly, her ethereal features clouding. "I'm afraid our peace may be tested by darker forces, my dear Nan," she said, her voice carrying the weight of untold years. A faint chill traced Nan's spine, and she clutched the skeleton key instinctively.

Nan leaned forward. "Whatever do you mean, Bithia? Surely nothing could dampen the excitement of having a bona fide Victorian spiritualist specter as a housemate!"

A rueful smile played across Bithia's translucent lips. "Oh, how I wish that were true. But I'm afraid there's more to my presence here than mere happenstance. You see, I'm trapped—not just by the confines of this mortal realm, but by a mystery that has haunted me since my untimely demise."

Nan furrowed her brow, her theatrical nature giving way to genuine concern. "Good heavens, trapped? That sounds positively dreadful. And here I thought the afterlife would be full of unlimited possibilities."

Bithia's laugh was like the tinkling of distant crystal. "No, I'm afraid something far more sinister lurks within these walls. A darkness that has terrorized not just me, but anyone who dares cross the threshold."

Nan's hand flew to her pearl necklace, clutching it reflexively, the key on the long silver chain swaying gently. "Goodness gracious! You don't mean to say we have a malevolent entity on our hands? And here I thought the most frightening thing about this house was the state of disrepair!"

"I'm afraid so," Bithia replied, her form shimmering with barely contained emotion. "I've been trying to uncover the truth behind my death and this haunting for longer than I care to admit. But I've been... limited in my efforts."

Nan stood up, pacing the room with nervous energy. "Well we simply can't have that, can we? A lady of your standing, stuck in limbo? It simply won't do!"

She turned to face Bithia, her eyes alight. "My dear Bithia, I vow to help you find peace and protect this house from whatever nefarious forces may be at work." Nan's voice softened, a rare seriousness settling over her usual cheer. "After all, we're both women who believe in the impossible, aren't we? You are on the other side, and I... well, I've always believed that stories—especially unfinished ones—are worth fighting for. We'll delve into historical records, dust off old tomes on spiritualism and, if need be, I'll learn to read tea leaves and work a planchette!"

Bithia's form seemed to brighten at Nan's words. "You would do that for me? For this house?"

"Of course!" Nan exclaimed, her voice rising. "What's a little supernatural sleuthing between friends? Besides, I've always fancied myself a bit of an amateur detective. Though I must admit, communicating with sinister entities wasn't quite what I had in mind when I dreamed of opening a B&B."

As Nan's words echoed through the room, she imagined what adventures lay ahead. And, more importantly, would she be able to unravel the mystery before whatever dark force lurking in the shadows made its presence known?

As Bithia began to speak, Nan found herself unconsciously leaning forward, hanging on every spectral word. The ghost's voice took on a more serious tone, "The entity that haunts this house is no mere bump-in-the-night specter, my dear. It's a malevolent force that has confounded even my considerable talents as a spiritualist."

Nan's mind raced with possibilities. What could be so formidable as to challenge a Victorian medium of Bithia's caliber imbued with all the powers of the afterlife? She voiced her thoughts aloud: "But surely, between your supernatural prowess and my mortal help, we stand a chance?"

Bithia's form flickered, a sad smile playing on her translucent lips. "Your optimism is admirable, Nan. It reminds me of my own fervor when I first began communing with the spirits. We may indeed stand a chance, but the risks..." She trailed off, her gaze distant.

Nan felt a warmth spreading through her chest, a fondness for this spectral woman from another time. "Well then," she said, straightening her dress with flourish, "we shall simply have to be extra clever, shan't we? After all, two heads are better than one. Even if one of them is, well, somewhat less corporeal than the other."

A ghostly chuckle escaped Bithia's lips. "Oh, my dear, you do have a way with words. Very well, let us embark on this perilous adventure together. Though I warn you, it may involve more than just rifling through dusty old tomes and hosting the occasional séance."

Nan tapped her finger on her lip. "I do think we start with rifling through dusty tomes. The attic would be a splendid place to start. After all, what self-respecting Victorian home doesn't keep its darkest secrets tucked away in the rafters?"

Bithia nodded, her form shimmering like gossamer in the golden afternoon light. "A keen observation, Mrs. Nettles. The attic has indeed been a repository of many curious artifacts over the years. Shall we ascend?"

As they made their way up the creaking stairs, Nan's mind

raced with possibilities. "I must say, Bithia, this is all terribly exciting. It's like stepping into one of my grandmother's beloved ghost stories, only with considerably less screaming and fainting."

Bithia's laughter echoed softly through the stairwell. "The day is still young. There may yet be time for a touch of Victorian dramatics."

Reaching the attic door Nan paused, her hand hovering over the tarnished brass knob. She took a deep breath, steeling herself for whatever lay beyond. "Well, here we go. Into the belly of the beast, as it were."

As she pushed open the door a gust of musty air rushed past, thick with the scent of mothballs and mildew. The wooden beams creaked overhead, as though the attic itself exhaled. The faint glow of sunlight filtering through a cracked window caught on cobwebs, their silken threads shimmering like ghostly veils.

Nan stepped inside, her eyes adjusting to the gloom. Dusty shapes loomed in the shadows, hinting at treasures waiting to be discovered.

"My word," Nan breathed, her voice barely above a whisper. "It's like a treasure trove of mysteries up here. Where should we start, Bithia?"

But as Nan turned to face her ghostly companion, she found only a wisp of light hovering near the ceiling before it faded entirely. The air crackled faintly, as though charged with static. "Bithia?" Nan called softly, the echoes of her voice swallowed by the attic's silence.

Bithia had vanished, leaving Nan surrounded by the remnants of the past.

"Bithia?" Nan called softly. "Have you gone and pulled a disappearing act on me already? And here I thought we were just getting started."

As she took her first tentative steps into the attic's depths, Nan smiled. "Well," she pondered to herself, "I suppose every good detective must learn to follow the clues on her own. Let's see what secrets this old house is hiding, shall we?"

Ghosts of the Garden

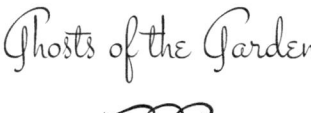

The afternoon sun draped the overgrown garden in warm, golden light, casting shadows that seemed to dance across the tangled greenery. Nan knelt in the dirt, her fingers curling around the stubborn stem of a weed that clung to the soil with surprising force.

"There now," she murmured, brushing soil from her hands. "That's one less interloper in my little Eden."

A faint hum filled the air. Not the buzz of insects but something deeper, as if the very earth beneath her hands held a pulse of its own.

As she surveyed the tangle of greenery before her, a cacophony of hammering and drilling erupted from within the house. She winced, furrowing her brow.

"Oh, Mossy, must you be so enthusiastic with your renovations?" she huffed, eyeing the Victorian home's weathered facade. "I do hope the spirits aren't too disturbed by all this commotion."

She returned her attention to the flower bed, methodically working her way through the weeds. Her mind wandered as she toiled, imagining how lovely the garden would look once restored to its former glory. Perhaps she'd plant some night-blooming jasmine, to entice nocturnal visitors—both corporeal and ethereal.

A particularly loud crash from inside the house startled Nan from her reverie. She sat back on her heels, brushing a stray curl from her forehead with the back of her hand.

"Mossy dear?" she called out. "Is everything quite all right in there?"

Her husband's muffled voice drifted through an open window. "Just peachy, darling! We're making marvelous progress! Just marvelous!"

Nan chuckled, shaking her head fondly. "Well, do try not to bring the whole house down around your ears. I'm rather attached to it, you know."

"The house, or my ears?" Mossy replied. " Don't worry, darling. I've got everything under control!"

No sooner had the words left his mouth than another tremendous crash resounded, followed by a chorus of alarmed shouts.

Nan sighed, turning back to her weeding. "Under control indeed," she brooded. "I do hope Bithia isn't too put out by all this hullabaloo."

As she worked Nan hummed a jaunty tune, determined to create an oasis of tranquility amidst the chaos. After all, what was a haunted Victorian bed and breakfast without a properly atmospheric garden?

Nan wiped her brow, surveying the overgrown expanse before her. The hurricane had left its mark, scattering palm fronds across the lawn like discarded fans at a ghostly ball. She set about gathering the debris.

"Well, now," she murmured to herself, hefting an armful of fronds. "I daresay we've made quite a mess of things, haven't we? But fear not, my leafy friends. We shall soon have you sorted."

As she stacked the fronds at the curb, a sense of accomplishment overwhelmed Nan. Each pile was a visual metaphor for the transformation of their Victorian lady from disheveled dowager to elegant hostess.

A glint of smooth stone caught Nan's eye, winking like a hidden jewel amidst the riot of green. Intrigued, she pushed aside the vines, her hands brushing against the cool, damp leaves. Slowly, an ornate fountain emerged, its edges softened by moss and time. Carved cherubs peered out from the stone, their faces weathered yet serene, as if waiting patiently for someone to notice them again. The discovery felt like unearthing a forgotten secret—a whisper of the house's past brought to light.

"Well, I never!" Nan exclaimed, her eyes widening. "What have we here? A secret garden, perhaps?"

As she cleared away more foliage a second fountain emerged, twin to the first. Nan's heart quickened with excitement.

"Mossy!" she called out. "You simply must come and see this!"

But the cacophony from inside the house drowned out her voice. Undeterred, Nan set about examining the fountains. To her delight she found them structurally sound, if a bit worse for wear.

"Now, then," she evaluated, running her fingers along the intricate stonework. "Let's see if we can't breathe some life back into you lovelies."

By fiddling with some tools and using water from the hose in the front yard, Nan was able to successfully encourage a small amount of water flow from the fountains. As the gentle sound filled the air she closed her eyes, imagining the garden as it once was—and as it would be again.

"There, now," she said softly, addressing the house and its unseen inhabitants. "That's much better, isn't it?"

The trickle of water from the newly revived fountains filled the air with a soothing melody. Nan stood back, admiring her handiwork with a satisfied smile. The sun's warmth caressed her face as she wiped her brow, leaving a smudge of dirt across her forehead.

The cheerful ding-ding of a bicycle bell pierced the tranquil atmosphere, followed by a melodious laugh that seemed to dance on the breeze. Nan turned to see a vision in peach and yellow pedaling towards her on a charming cruiser bicycle, its wicker basket overflowing with vibrant blooms.

"Hullo there, neighbor!" The voice rang out like a melody, warm and lilting as its owner pedaled into view, her wide-brimmed sun hat bobbing with each turn of the pedals. "I do hope I'm not intruding on your gardening reverie! Mabel Hughes, at your service," she declared, dismounting with surprising grace considering her ample figure. "Official neighborhood greeter and purveyor of floral goodwill."

Nan brushed her hands down the front of her gardening apron. "Not at all! I'm Nan Nettles, the new proprietress of this delightful, if somewhat overgrown, establishment. It's lovely to make your acquaintance, Mabel!"

"Oh, Mrs. Nettles! Welcome to our little slice of paradise! Please don't be offended if you find yourself without too many visitors. I'm afraid this property has quite the reputation."

"Do call me Nan. No need for formalities." Nan smiled. "As to the property's reputation, we are hoping that with love and elbow grease we can give this old girl a second chance. I dare say, when we are through with her she will be the belle of the ball."

Mabel presented Nan with a stunning bouquet. "A little housewarming gift, chosen with the utmost care and consideration for their Victorian symbolism."

Nan gently caressed the delicate petals. "How perfectly splendid! I've always been fascinated by the language of flowers. Do tell, what secrets do these beauties hold?"

Mabel's eyes twinkled with delight. "Ah, my dear, you've stumbled upon a treasure trove of enchantment! Each bloom carries a message from the fairy realm itself."

Nan leaned in, captivated. "Do go on, Mabel. I'm all ears for a touch of whimsy and wonder."

"Well," Mabel began, her voice taking on a lyrical quality, "these lavender roses speak of love at first sight—perhaps between you and this charming abode? The forget-me-nots nestled among them whisper of true love and memories."

Nan's thoughts drifted to the spectral figure of Bithia she'd encountered. "How fitting," she murmured. "This house does seem to be brimming with memories."

Mabel continued, unaware of Nan's momentary distraction. "And this sprig of rosemary is for remembrance," Mabel said, holding it aloft like a magician revealing a spell. "While the delicate baby's breath whispers of everlasting love."

"My word," Nan breathed, her theatrical nature coming to the fore. "It's as if you've woven a spell with these blossoms, Mabel. I half expect to see fairies dancing among the petals!"

Mabel's laughter rang out once more. "Who's to say they aren't, my friend? The veil between our world and theirs is thin in places like this, where history and mystery intertwine."

Nan's heart swelled with delight. Here, at last, was someone who understood the magic that seemed to permeate every corner of her new home. "Oh, Mabel," she said, her voice filled with warmth. "I do believe we will be the best of friends."

Nan and Mabel settled onto the porch swing, the bouquet nestled between them like a vibrant promise of camaraderie. The gentle creaking of the swing mingled with the distant crash of ocean waves, creating a soothing rhythm that seemed to draw the women closer.

"Do tell me all about yourself, Mabel!" Nan leaned in, anxious to hear every word.

The woman spoke with a gentle lilt as she shared her story. "There's not much to say," she began. "I own the sweet little flower shop off of Granada, where vibrant blooms and fragrant scents fill the air. My dear husband, God rest his soul, left this world several years ago." A wistful sigh escaped her lips before she continued, "And ever since then, I've noticed cats mysteriously appear wherever I go. I have a feeling that my late husband sends them to me to keep me company in his absence." She chuckled and her smile widened, revealing a gap between her teeth. As she spoke, a black and white cat emerged from behind a pot of pink petunias and rubbed against her leg affectionately. "See, they find me no matter where I go. Are you fond of cats?"

"I'm more of a dog lady myself, but felines are divine," Nan cooed as she bent down to pet the cat.

"I must say, Mabel," Nan began, her eyes flashing with mirth, "I know we just met, but it feels as though we've known each other for ages. Perhaps we were acquainted in a past life? I could easily picture us as a pair of mischievous Victorian ladies, sneaking off to séances and scandalizing the town."

Mabel's laughter bubbled up like champagne. "Oh, Nan! What a delightful notion. I can almost see us now, all corseted and crinolined, tiptoeing through gas-lit streets."

As their giggles subsided, Nan found herself pondering the house looming behind them. Its weathered facade seemed to hold countless secrets, whispering just beyond her comprehension. "Speaking of Victorian intrigue," she ventured, "I don't suppose you know any juicy tales about this grand old dame?"

Mabel's eyes widened, trepidation flickering across her face. "Oh my, where to begin?" She leaned in conspiratorially. "They say this house has seen its fair share of... otherworldly visitors. Specters of the Victorian Era trailing silk and sorrow." She paused for effect, then added with a grin, "Or perhaps it's just old plumbing. Either way it makes a fabulous story, doesn't it?"

A breeze rustled through the garden, cool and oddly fragrant, carrying the faintest trace of lavender. Nan felt a delicious shiver run down her spine. "Do tell, darling. I'm positively aquiver with curiosity."

"Well," Mabel began, her voice dropping to a dramatic whisper, "legend has it that on certain nights, when the moon is full and the sea mist rolls in, ethereal music can be heard drifting from the attic. And more than one neighbor has sworn they've seen a woman in Victorian dress gazing forlornly from that very window."

Nan's heart quickened, her thoughts immediately flying to Bithia. "How utterly thrilling," she murmured, careful not to reveal her own ghostly encounter. "And what of this spirit? Is she believed to be friendly, or... otherwise?"

Mabel's expression grew somber. "Ah, there's the rub, my dear. Some say she's a benevolent presence, guiding lost souls. Others whisper of a vengeful spirit, wronged in life and seeking retribution in death."

As Mabel spoke, Nan cast a furtive glance towards the attic window. For a moment, she thought she saw a flicker of movement behind the dusty pane. "Goodness," she breathed. "It seems I've inherited quite the enigma along with this charming B&B."

Nan's fingers traced the delicate pearl necklace on her neck, a nervous habit she'd developed over the years. She became aware of the weight of the key that hung near her heart. She took a deep breath, the scent of jasmine from the garden mingling with the salty sea air. "Mabel, darling," she began, her voice taking on a theatrical whisper, "I must confess something rather... extraordinary."

Mabel leaned in, her eyes wide with curiosity beneath her wide-brimmed sun hat. "Oh? Do tell, Nan. I'm all ears, as they say."

Nan's gaze darted around, as if checking for eavesdroppers among the newly revived fountains. "You see, I've had a rather... intimate encounter with our spectral resident." She paused, gauging Mabel's reaction. "The ghost you spoke of is quite real, I assure you. Her name is Bithia."

Mabel's soft features registered surprise, but not disbelief. "Gracious me! You've seen her?"

"More than seen, dear friend," Nan continued, gesticulating animatedly. "We've spoken. She's... well, she's quite the character. Frighteningly Victorian in her sensibilities, but with a wit as sharp as a tack."

As Nan recounted her ghostly tête-à-tête Mabel listened with rapt attention, her expression shifting between awe and intrigue. "How utterly fascinating," she breathed. "And here I thought my garden gnomes coming to life was the height of supernatural excitement!"

Nan chuckled at Mabel's quip, feeling a surge of affection for her new friend. "Oh, Mabel, I do hope you'll join me in this quest. There's so much to uncover about Bithia's past, her untimely demise, and why she's trapped in this particular abode. Will you help me solve this spectral mystery?"

Mabel's eyes lit up with excitement. "My dear Nan, while I've never had the pleasure of ghostly company myself, I wouldn't miss this for the world. Count me in!"

As Mabel spoke, a gentle breeze rustled through the garden, carrying with it the faintest whisper of ethereal laughter.

Nan beamed, clasping Mabel's hands in her own. "Oh, splendid! I do believe we'll make a formidable team. Shall we convene for tea tomorrow afternoon? We can pore over the house's history and devise our plan of action."

Mabel nodded enthusiastically, her sun hat bobbing. "A capital idea, Nan! I'll bring my grandmother's scrapbook—it's filled with local lore that might prove useful. If I'm not mistaken, I believe she attended some of the séances back in her day. Shall we say four o'clock?"

"Four o'clock it is," Nan agreed.

Mabel smiled. "I'll bring some sticky buns. I daresay even Bithia might be tempted to join us for those!"

As Mabel pedaled away on her cruiser bicycle, the sound of her tinkling laughter lingering in the air, Nan turned back to her gardening with renewed vigor. She knelt among the overgrown flower beds, her fingers working deftly to free delicate blooms from choking weeds.

How curious, Nan mused, *to find oneself so deeply invested in the affairs of the deceased.* She paused, chuckling at the absurdity of it all. *If only my dear grandmother could see me now, up to my elbows in dirt and ghostly intrigue!*

As she worked Nan felt an inexplicable pull towards the house, as if its very walls were whispering secrets only she could hear. The Victorian manor loomed behind her, its weathered façade a silent witness to decades of hidden histories.

We'll get to the bottom of this, old girl, Nan thought, patting the earth affectionately. *You, me, Mabel, and our spectral friend upstairs. What a quirky quartet we'll make!*

On impulse Nan glanced up at the attic window, half-expecting to see Bithia's translucent form. Instead, her breath hitched. A dark, formless shadow loomed in the attic window, rippling like smoke but impossibly still. It seemed to pulse, radiating a cold energy that froze the air around her. For a fleeting moment, she thought she saw eyes—glinting, hollow, and watching.

"Good heavens!" Nan gasped, scrambling backwards. The

shadow seemed to pulse with otherworldly energy, growing larger and more ominous by the second.

Terror gripped Nan's heart as she stared transfixed at the nightmarish apparition. *Oh, Bithia*, she thought frantically, *what have you gotten me into?*

Tea and Secrets

The sun-drenched porch of Nettles' B&B shimmered like a polished pearl, its gingerbread finials and sawn balusters casting intricate lace-like shadows. A faint breeze carried the mingling scents of jasmine and salt air, whispering through the twin fountains and setting the ferns trembling, as if the grounds itself were breathing softly. Nan settled into a wicker rocking chair, feeling rather like Alice tumbling into Wonderland—if Wonderland had been a Victorian seaside resort with a penchant for supernatural occurrences.

"I do declare, Mabel," Nan said over the babbling of the twin fountains, blinking rapidly, "if this porch gets any whiter, we'll need sunglasses just to sip our tea. The new coat of paint has done this old girl wonders."

Mabel's laugh tinkled like wind chimes as she placed a basket on the circular table between them. "Oh, Nan! The house is looking marvelous. Speaking of tea, I've brought you a little something to sweeten our ghostly investigations."

Nan closed her eyes in rapture. "Thank you Mabel, the kitchen is in such disarray. I have been doing all the basic cooking in the RV."

"Oh?" Mabel questioned, scanning the garden but finding no sign of a recreational vehicle.

"It's hidden in the rear corner of the back yard, thanks to Mossy's clever placement. It blends in perfectly beneath the weeping willow!" She chuckled.

A rhythmic thumping from above drew Nan's gaze upward. There, precariously balanced half out of the attic window, was Mossy, his hair ruffling in the breeze as he called out instructions to the workers on the roof.

Nan's heart swelled with pride. "Would you look at that?" she mused aloud. "My Mossy, orchestrating this renovation like a maestro conducting a symphony of hammers and nails."

"He's doing a fabulous job," Mabel agreed, her eyes widening as she took in the freshly planted rose garden. "And you, my dear! Your green thumb has worked wonders. Those roses look positively enchanted."

Nan beamed, her fingers absently tracing the pearls on her wrist. "Why, thank you, Mabel. I'm rather pleased with how they've turned out. They were shipped over from England— David Austin's roses. My first shipment."

"Simply divine," Mabel swooned.

"Next on my list is the herb garden. I'm thinking a touch of rosemary and thyme might help ward off any unfriendly spirits."

"If not the spirits, at least the mosquitoes." Mabel chuckled. "Speaking of spirits," Mabel started, leaning in, her voice dropping to a conspiratorial whisper, "have you had any more nocturnal visits from our dear Bithia?"

Nan sighed, a mix of disappointment and relief coloring her words. "Not a peep, I'm afraid. The only ghostly sounds in the night have been Mossy's thunderous snores. I swear, sometimes I think he's trying to communicate with the spirit world through the power of his nasal passages."

As they shared a laugh, Nan felt a twinge of unease. No

sign of Bithia yet, but something was in the air—besides the scent of her new apricot blooms and sea salt, and the distant echo of hammering from the roof.

The wicker chair creaked as Nan rose, her floral apron swishing softly. "Now, then, Mabel dear, shall we fortify ourselves for our foray into the past? The kitchen can handle making a spot of tea." She disappeared into the house, returning moments later with a gleaming silver tea service complete with tiny plates and napkins for Mabel's sticky buns.

"Here's to peeling back the layers of the past," Nan declared, her teacup poised in mid-air as if toasting an unseen audience. The Earl Grey, a symphony of bergamot and black tea, flowed down her throat.

"Earl Grey indeed," Mabel confirmed with a nod. "A bit of liquid courage for our quest."

Mabel then unveiled the sticky buns she had brought along. Their aroma wafted through the air, a bouquet of gooey sweetness underscored by buttery undertones. She placed one on each plate with a flourish that spoke volumes about her pride in these baked masterpieces.

As Nan took a bite, it was as if time stood still. The bun melted delicately between her teeth, releasing waves of buttery goodness laced with cinnamon's subtle perfume. The tender interior melted on her tongue like morning dew on petals.

Her eyes closed in sheer bliss as she savored the harmony of flavors playing out in her mouth, the earthy notes of nutmeg dancing gracefully over the rich canvas of butter and flour. A sigh escaped from between her lips before she could stifle it. This was more than just eating; it was an experience that transcended mere sustenance.

"Mabel," Nan breathed out finally when words returned to her. "These are divine." She opened her eyes to find Mabel beaming at the compliment.

Mabel laughed lightly, tucking a stray curl behind her ear

as she explained how she'd experimented with different amounts of cinnamon and caramel until she found just the right balance—enough to give them a distinctive sweetness without overpowering the subtle hints of vanilla.

"To think they were just ordinary dough this morning," Mabel mused aloud, casting an affectionate glance at the remaining buns. "And now they're part of our mystery-solving ritual. Quite a transformation, wouldn't you say?"

Mabel carefully spread out a collection of yellowed newspaper clippings and faded photographs on the table. "Shall we begin our descent into the rabbit hole of history, my dear Sherlock?" she asked with a playful wink.

Nan chuckled, adjusting her reading glasses. "Elementary, my dear Mabel. Though I daresay our dear Bithia's exploits might give even Sherlock a run for his money."

As they leaned in to examine the documents, Nan felt a familiar thrill of excitement. Her fingers, slightly trembling, gently traced the edges of a particularly intriguing photograph.

"Oh my," she breathed, her eyes widening. "Mabel, look at this! It's Bithia, clear as day, conducting what appears to be a rather dramatic séance."

Mabel peered closer, her brow furrowed. "Indeed, and if I'm not mistaken, that stern-looking woman in the corner... could that be her sister?"

Nan nodded, her mind racing. "It must be. The family resemblance is unmistakable, though that lady looks about as pleased as a cat in a rainstorm. I can't help but wonder if there was a rift between the sisters."

Mabel's eyes flashed with excitement as she reached into her wicker basket, producing a leather-bound tome with gilded edges. "Nan, feast your eyes upon this treasure trove of history past!"

Nan leaned forward, her curiosity piqued. "My word, Mabel! Is that—"

"My grandmother's scrapbook," Mabel confirmed, gently placing it on the table. "A veritable encyclopedia of the town's history, including Bithia's spiritual exploits."

As they carefully turned the fragile pages, Nan's breath caught in her throat. "Good heavens! Is that Sir Arthur Conan Doyle?"

Mabel nodded enthusiastically. "The very same! Oh, to have been a fly on the wall during that séance."

Nan sighed wistfully. "Can you imagine? The creator of Sherlock Holmes, communing with spirits in my very own humble home?"

As they continued to peruse the photographs, a pattern emerged. Nan furrowed her brow. "Mabel, do you notice anything peculiar about Bithia's sister in these images?"

Mabel squinted. "Why, she looks positively thunderous in every shot! As if she's trying to bore holes through Bithia with her eyes alone."

Nan nodded, a knot forming in her stomach. "I can't help but wonder what sort of relationship the sisters had. It seems far from sisterly affection, doesn't it?"

Their musings were interrupted by a rustling of papers. Mabel produced a yellowed newspaper clipping, her expression grave. "Nan, dear, I'm afraid I've found something rather... unsettling."

Nan leaned in, her heart quickening. "What is it, Mabel?"

"It appears your charming abode has a darker history than we realized," Mabel said, her voice trembling slightly. She held up a faded clipping, the edges brittle with age. "These articles speak of a malevolent presence—a revenant, they call it."

As if in response, a chill breeze swept across the porch, setting the ferns quivering. Nan shivered, pulling her shawl tighter around her shoulders. "A revenant?" she repeated, her voice barely a whisper. "I'm afraid my knowledge of spectral taxonomy is somewhat lacking."

Mabel's voice dropped to a whisper. "It's a particularly nasty sort of spirit, my dear. One bent on terrorizing the living and the dead, fueled by rage and unfinished business."

Nan's teacup trembled slightly in her hand as she processed the information.

"Mabel," she said softly, "how many... incidents are we talking about?"

Her friend's face was grim. "Far too many, I'm afraid. The reports span decades—mysterious accidents, unexplained illnesses, even deaths."

Nan's heart sank as she stared at the article in Mabel's hands. The charming Victorian home she'd fallen in love with was undeniably cloaked in shadow, its gingerbread trim and cheerful paint masking decades of sorrow. But as the initial wave of dread passed, she straightened her shoulders. "If Bithia is staying to fight, then so am I," she said firmly. "This house deserves peace, and I intend to see it through."

"Oh, Mabel," she whispered, her voice quavering. "We just have to find a way."

Nan widened her eyes as she leaned forward, her pearl bracelet clinking softly against her teacup. "But Mabel, if this revenant is so terribly wicked, why would dear Bithia remain? Surely she'd want to escape such a malevolent presence."

Mabel tilted her head, causing her oversized sun hat to cast a whimsical shadow across her face. "Perhaps, my dear, it's not a matter of want but of need. Like a delicate rose tethered to its thorny stem."

Nan pondered this, her fingers absently tracing the rim of her cup. "You don't suppose... could Bithia be protecting us from this revenant somehow?"

"Oh!" Mabel exclaimed, her eyes lighting with excitement. "What if she's locked in an eternal spiritual battle, like a ghostly game of chess? Bithia as the white queen, defending against the dark forces?"

Nan chuckled at her friend's fanciful imagery. She felt a familiar prickle at the nape of her neck, the same sensation she experienced when she first met Bithia. "My dear Mabel, Bithia seems to have made protecting this house her mission. I think she sees herself as its guardian." The odd sensation lingered for a moment before fading, leaving Nan with the oddest sense of reassurance.

"You know," Nan mused, her voice dropping to a conspiratorial whisper, "I can't help but wonder if Bithia and this revenant might be... connected somehow. Two sides of the same spectral coin, as it were."

Mabel swayed slowly in her rocking chair, her eyes veiled with intrigue. "Oh, Nan! What a deliciously eerie thought. We simply must investigate further." She reached into her floral-print handbag, producing a leather-bound notebook and a rather ornate fountain pen.

Nan couldn't suppress a fond smile at her friend's enthusiasm. "Quite right, my dear. Let's jot down our burning questions, shall we?"

As Mabel poised her pen over the crisp page Nan began to pace, her heels clicking a rhythmic dance on the freshly painted porch. "First and foremost, we must ascertain when and how our dear Bithia shed this mortal coil. The circumstances of her death may hold the key to her... current predicament."

"Excellent point." Mabel nodded, her pen scratching across the paper. "And what of the last residents? Did they flee in terror from this nefarious revenant, or was their departure more mundane?"

Nan paused, gazing out at the setting sun. Its warm glow bathed the garden in a melancholy light, lending an air of mystery to their conversation. "I do wonder," she mused, "if there might be some connection between Bithia's séances and the revenant's appearance. Could she have inadvertently summoned something beyond her control?"

As they continued their discussion, the golden light deepened to a rich amber. The distant sound of hammering ceased, followed by the shuffling of work boots on the roof. Nan turned to see the construction workers making their way down the ladders, tools in hand.

"Good evening, gentlemen!" Nan called out, her voice warm and inviting. "I do hope you'll have a wonderful evening. I do greatly appreciate all of your excellent work."

The workers tipped their hats, bidding farewell with good-natured smiles. As they departed, Nan felt a swell of pride in her beloved Nettles' B&B. Even half-finished, it exuded a charm that seemed to captivate all who dared crossed its threshold.

"You know, Mabel," Nan said, turning back to her friend with a mischievous smile on her lips, "I rather think we're on to something quite extraordinary here. A Victorian spiritualist, a malevolent revenant, and a bed and breakfast with more secrets than a dowager's diary. It's positively delightful."

Mabel set her teacup down, her round face alight with excitement. "Oh, Nan, I couldn't agree more! It's as if we've stumbled into one of those penny dreadfuls, only far more thrilling." She clasped Nan's hand, her touch warm and reassuring. "We simply must see this through to the end."

Nan felt a surge of affection for her new friend. "Indeed, we shall, my dear Mabel. I propose we make a solemn pact, here and now." She raised her teacup, the last dregs of Earl Grey swirling at the bottom. "To uncover the truth about Bithia and banish this dreadful revenant, come what may."

"Oh, how perfectly dramatic!" Mabel exclaimed, seizing her own cup and raising it with a flourish. "I swear by all the flowers in my garden and the spirits that may lurk therein, I shall stand by your side through every spectral encounter and dusty archive."

"My dear Mabel," Nan said, setting down her cup with a gentle clink, "I do believe we've embarked on a most singular adventure. One that would make even the great Sherlock Holmes raise an intrigued eyebrow."

Mabel giggled, her laughter like tinkling bells in the gathering twilight. "Oh, wouldn't that be something? Perhaps we should invest in a pair of deerstalker caps and magnifying glasses."

As the last rays of sunlight faded, spilling shades of purples and salmon across the sky, Nan felt a reluctance to end their delightful evening. Yet the encroaching darkness signaled that she needed to tend to Mossy. No doubt he had many a tale to tell about his day.

"I suppose we should call it an evening." Nan sighed, rising from her chair. "But let's reconvene soon, shall we? I've a feeling our ghostly residents won't keep us waiting long for the next clue."

Mabel nodded, gathering her belongings. "Oh, absolutely! I'll bring my grandmother's old spirit board next time. Who knows? We might just coax some answers out of the ether itself!"

As they bid each other farewell, Nan wondered what unseen eyes might be watching from the shadowy corners. The night ahead felt to be anything but ordinary, and she found herself oddly thrilled by the prospect.

Nan stood at the edge of the porch, her hand resting lightly on the freshly painted railing as she watched Mabel pedal away on her cruiser bicycle. The whimsical sight of her friend, sun hat bobbing and wicker basket swaying, brought a fond smile to Nan's lips.

"Do be careful, Mabel dear!" Nan called out, her voice

carrying a hint of theatrical concern. "One never knows what spectral shenanigans might be afoot after sunset!"

Mabel's laughter drifted back, mingling with the gentle creaking of her bicycle. "Fear not, Nan! I've stuffed my pockets with lavender. No self-respecting ghost would dare accost a lady so aromatic!"

As Mabel disappeared around the corner, Nan found herself alone on the porch, enveloped by the soft embrace of twilight. She sank into one of the white wicker chairs, letting out a contented sigh as she allowed herself a few moments of contemplation alone.

"Well, Bithia," Nan murmured to the empty air, "I do hope you approve of our little investigation. Though I must say your taste in houseguests leaves something to be desired. A revenant, indeed!"

Just then the faint strains of jazz began to drift through an open window, the melancholy notes of a saxophone weaving through the evening stillness. Nan closed her eyes, allowing the music to wash over her.

"How curious," she mused, frowning slightly. "I don't recall leaving any music playing. Perhaps our spectral residents have developed a taste for Louis Armstrong?"

A wry smile tugged at her lips as she thought about it. How odd it was that she had gone from wondering about the different states they would visit in their Mossy Mobile, to settling down for extended periods of time in their Key West home, to now being the owner of a B&B in Daytona Beach of all places. Yet, as she sat there, she realized she was completely content and at ease with her new life.

"Well," she said softly to herself, "if one must share a home with ghosts, I suppose it's only fitting they have good taste in music."

As the last strains of jazz faded, a faint knock echoed from the far end of the porch. Nan's breath caught. Slowly she turned toward the sound, but nothing was there—just the swaying shadows of the ferns in the moonlight.

The creak of the screen door heralded Mossy's arrival, his hair gleaming like a halo in the dim light.

"My dearest," he intoned, his voice rich with affection, "I come bearing a pre-dinner libation to enjoy with the lady of the house." In his hands, two crystal tumblers winked with amber liquid.

Nan's heart fluttered at the sight of her husband. "Mossy, you romantic old fool," she said fondly, watching as he set the glasses down on the table beside her.

Before she could reach for her drink Mossy's hand was extended towards her, an invitation in his eyes. "May I have this dance, my love?"

"Oh, Mossy," Nan protested, even as she allowed him to pull her to her feet.

Mossy chuckled, drawing her close. "The lady doth protest too much."

As they began to sway to the slow jazz, Nan found herself transported. The crickets provided a gentle percussion to accompany the music drifting from inside, and above them the stars twinkled like a thousand watchful eyes.

"Do you think Bithia approves of our dancing?" Nan whispered, her cheek resting against Mossy's chest.

"My darling," Mossy replied, his voice rumbling beneath her ear, "if our spectral housemate objects to a bit of romance, I dare say she's been dead far too long."

Nan laughed, the sound mingling with the music and the night air. As Mossy twirled her, her sundress flaring out around her, Nan felt a profound sense of rightness settle over her. Ghosts, Revenants, and mysteries be damned. In this moment all was perfectly, wonderfully right with the world.

The Revenant's Shadow

Mabel leaned her vintage cruiser bike against the newly placed white picket fence that enclosed the Nettles' Bed and Breakfast. She admired the way the sunlight shone through the gaps, casting beautiful shadows on the velvety grass below. It was as if she had stepped into a fairytale, nestled in the heart of the seaside town.

She lifted her gaze to the roof where a group of workers was still busy with the dormers and new fish scale shingles. From this angle, they almost looked like animated gargoyles. She could hear Mr. Nettles' voice echoing in the background as he asked questions, but despite scanning each window she couldn't spot his figure. However, from one particular window in the attic, there appeared to be a shadow or blur. She narrowed her eyes and shook her head. Was her imagination playing tricks on her, or did she really see something?

Nan flung open the door, her face lighting up at the sight of her friend. "Mabel, you absolute vision of a summer's day!" she exclaimed, pulling the shorter woman into a warm embrace.

Mabel's sun-kissed face crinkled with laughter, her button

nose wrinkling adorably. "Oh, Nan, you flatterer! I've brought a little surprise for our spiritualist soirée," she said, her eyes glittering with delight.

Nan's heart fluttered with excitement as she ushered Mabel into the newly renovated parlor. The room was a symphony of dark, rich colors and ornate velvet furnishings, a perfect blend of French Rococo revival and Victorian opulence. Nan watched with glee as Mabel's eyes widened, taking in the shield-back armchair, the grand lady's chair, and the imposing grandfather clock that stood sentinel in the corner.

"Nan, you've outdone yourself!" Mabel gasped, her fingers trailing reverently over the etagere. "It's like stepping into a scene from one of those delicious gothic novels we adore."

Nan preened inwardly, pleased by her friend's reaction. "Well, my dear, one must set the proper stage for communing with the spirits, mustn't one?" She gestured towards the sofa, where a tray of steaming vanilla chai and freshly baked chocolate almond biscotti awaited them. "Now, tell me about this surprise of yours."

As they settled onto the plush velvet, Mabel reached into her wicker basket and produced an intricately carved wooden board. "My grandmother's spirit board," she announced with a flourish. "I thought it might add a touch of authenticity to our research."

Nan ran her fingers over the smooth surface of the board. "Oh, Mabel, it's perfect! Just imagine the secrets it might reveal about dear Bithia's past."

The two women excitedly discussed their recent findings on Victorian-era spiritualism, nibbling on biscotti and sipping chai. Maybe tonight would finally be the night when Bithia would make an appearance. Nan had only made contact the one time.

Their fervent discussion was interrupted by the sound of

measured footsteps. Mossy appeared in the doorway, brushing his hands down the front of his trousers and wiping away dust as he peered at them over his thin spectacles.

"My dear, I do believe this is your friend Mabel," he greeted with a friendly smile. "It's a pleasure to make your acquaintance."

"Likewise, Mr. Nettles. You are truly doing wonders with this old house," Mabel replied warmly.

His gaze fell upon the spirit board, and Nan could almost see the gears of skepticism turning in his mind.

Mossy crossed his arms, an amused glint in his eyes. "Ah, an amateur production of *Ghosts of the Parlor*. Shall I fetch a monocle to complete the Victorian vibe?" He paused, choosing his words carefully. "While I admire your enthusiasm, my dear Nan, perhaps it might be more prudent to focus on more earthly matters? A safe perusal of the local library, perhaps? I worry about your safety in these... spiritual pursuits."

Nan felt a pang of guilt at her husband's words, but the allure of the unknown was too strong to resist. "Oh, Mossy, you dear, practical man," she said, rising to plant a kiss on his cheek. "It always takes you a bit longer to embrace the supernatural. I promise we'll be careful. Besides, what harm could come from a little chat with the spirits? And in daylight no less?"

A chill breeze swept through the room as she spoke, causing the candles' flames to flicker ominously. Nan suppressed a shiver of excitement. Was it just the wind, or perhaps something more... otherworldly?

Nan exchanged a glance with Mabel, their eyes glittering with barely contained exhilaration. The spirit board lay before them, its polished surface gleaming in the soft candlelight.

"My dear Mossy," Nan said, her voice tinged with affectionate exasperation, "your concern is touching, but I'm afraid we simply must proceed. The spirits are practically beckoning us!"

Mabel nodded enthusiastically, her sun hat bobbing. "Oh yes, I can feel it in my bones! My grandmother always said that when the veil between worlds grows thin, it's our duty to listen."

Mossy sighed, shaking his head. "Very well, ladies. But do be careful. I'll be working on the plumbing upstairs if you need me—preferably for something less... ethereal."

As Mossy's footsteps faded, Nan turned to Mabel with a conspiratorial grin. "Shall we begin?"

Together, they moved to the center table of the parlor. Nan's heart raced as she arranged candles around the spirit board, her fingers trembling.

"Oh, Mabel," she whispered. "Can you feel it? The air seems... different somehow."

Mabel nodded, her eyes wide. "Like electricity, but softer. It reminds me of the way my garden feels just before a summer storm."

As they settled on either side of the spirit board, Nan admired how the flickering candlelight transformed the room. Shadows danced across the velvet furnishings and the grandfather clock's steady ticking seemed to fade into the background, as if time itself was holding its breath.

"Now," Nan said, her voice barely above a whisper, "let's invite the spirits to join us. Ready to summon the past, darling? Let's see if these spirits are as dramatic as Victorian novels claim."

Nan and Mabel exchanged a nervous glance before placing their fingertips delicately on the planchette. The polished wood felt cool beneath Nan's touch.

"We open our hearts and minds to the spirits of this house," Nan intoned, her voice steady despite the flutter in her stomach. "If there are any souls who wish to communicate, please make your presence known."

Mabel's eyes were closed, her brow furrowed in concentration. "I feel... something," she murmured. "Like a whisper just beyond hearing."

Nan nodded, though Mabel couldn't see. "Focus on that feeling, dear. Let it guide—"

Her words caught in her throat as a sudden chill swept through the room. The candle flames dipped and swayed, casting eerie, elongated shadows across the walls. The air thickened, cool and electric, as a faint, discordant melody emerged from nowhere, each note trembling like a plucked thread in the fabric of reality. It was as though an unseen orchestra was tuning their instruments, their dissonance echoing from some distant, unreachable place.

"Good heavens," Nan breathed, her eyes darting around the room. "Mabel, are you—"

"I'm all right," Mabel whispered, though her face had gone pale. "But Nan, look at the planchette!"

Nan glanced down to see the wooden pointer trembling beneath their fingers, eager to move of its own accord. A thrill of excitement tinged with just a hint of fear raced through her.

"Well," she said, forcing a lightness into her tone that she didn't quite feel, "it seems we have a guest. Shall we say hello?"

The planchette's trembling intensified, and Nan felt a chill creep up her spine as the room's atmosphere shifted dramatically. The ornate grandfather clock in the corner caught her eye, its hands spinning counterclockwise with alarming speed.

"Oh my," Nan gasped, her voice barely above a whisper. "Mabel, dear, I don't think we're dealing with a friendly spirit here."

Mabel's eyes widened as she took in the scene. "Nan, look at the curtains!"

The thick velvet drapes began to thrash violently, as if

caught in a tempest, despite the closed windows. The crystal chandelier above them swung in wild, erratic arcs, its delicate pendants tinkling ominously.

"Perhaps," Nan said, trying to keep her voice steady, "we should consider ending this séance before—"

A faint, melodious voice brushed past them, soft as a lullaby but impossible to ignore. Nan froze, catching the whisper of her name. "Did you hear that?" she asked, her voice tinged with awe. Before Mabel could answer, Bithia's sophisticated form emerged like moonlight spilling into the room.

"I see her! I see her!" Mabel proclaimed while pointing at the apparition.

"Bithia!" Nan exclaimed, relief flooding her voice. "Thank goodness you're here. We seem to have attracted some rather... unpleasant company."

Bithia's spectral form moved gracefully between Nan and Mabel and the unseen malevolent presence. When she spoke her voice was like a whisper on the wind. "My dears, you must be cautious. The revenant grows stronger, feeding on your fear and curiosity."

Mabel, who was overwhelmed with joy by the sight of Bithia, exclaimed excitedly, "The revenant? Is that what's causing all this commotion?"

"Indeed." Bithia nodded solemnly. "It is a spirit of great anger and jealousy; one I had hoped would never trouble you, Nan."

Nan's mind raced, torn between fascination and fear. "But why now? Why here?"

"Because, my dear," Bithia intoned, her form flickering slightly, "it has awakened. The spirit board is a powerful tool, but also a dangerous one in inexperienced hands."

A low growl resonated through the room. The flames on the candles wavered, shrinking to faint embers before vanishing altogether, leaving only the oppressive scent of sulfur and lavender. Shadows lengthened unnaturally, pooling in corners like inky predators waiting to pounce.

"Well," Nan said, forcing a wry smile, "I don't suppose you have any advice on how to politely show our uninvited guest the door?"

The air crackled with malevolent energy as the revenant's fury reached a crescendo. The delicate china tea set on the nearby etagere began to tremble, slowly rising in the air. Nan watched in horrified fascination as her prized Wedgwood teacups danced an eerie waltz mid-air.

"Oh, for heaven's sake," Nan muttered, her fingers tightening on the planchette. "Those were a wedding gift from Aunt Petunia."

Mabel, her round face pale, leaned in close. "Nan, darling, perhaps we should focus less on the china and more on the angry spirit trying to redecorate your parlor."

As if in response, the room began to shake violently, the French Rococo revival furniture skittering across the polished wooden floor. The grandfather clock in the corner let out a mournful bong, its pendulum swinging wildly.

Nan closed her eyes, drawing a deep breath. "Right, then. Let's see if we can't have a civil conversation with our spectral visitor, shall we?"

She focused her attention on the spirit board, her voice clear and steady despite the chaos surrounding them. "We mean you no harm. We seek only to understand. Will you communicate with us?"

For a moment the shaking intensified, and Nan feared they had only provoked the revenant further. But then, slowly, the planchette beneath their fingers began to move.

"M-A-B-E-L," Nan spelled out, frowning. "Mabel, I do believe it's addressing you directly."

Mabel's eyes widened, her breath quickened. "Me? But why would it—oh!"

The planchette jerked violently, nearly pulling their hands off the board. It skittered across the letters, spelling out a chilling message: "LEAVE HER ALONE."

Nan felt a chill but she steeled herself, set on maintaining their tenuous connection. "Now see here," she addressed the unseen presence, her voice taking on the stern tone she usually reserved for unruly guests. "There's no need for such dramatics. We're all civilized beings here, living or otherwise. Perhaps if you'd care to explain your grievances in a more genteel manner, we might reach an amicable solution."

As if in response to Nan's admonishment, the air around them shimmered and pulsed. The parlor erupted with a cacophony of ethereal forms, their translucent figures swirling in a dizzying dance around Nan and Mabel. Spectral faces contorted in anguish, mouths agape in silent screams that somehow pierced the very fabric of reality.

Nan's heart raced but she maintained her composure, her fingers still lightly resting on the planchette. "Well, I dare say we've drawn quite the crowd," she quipped, her voice only slightly trembling. "Mabel, dear, are you all right?"

Mabel, her sun-kissed face now pale as moonlight, nodded shakily. "I'm fine, Nan. But... goodness, there are so many of them!"

Just then Bithia's fashionable form materialized beside them, her presence a beacon of calm amidst the spectral storm. Nan felt a surge of relief at the sight of her ghostly friend.

"Bithia," Nan breathed. "We're ever so glad to see you. These spirits... they seem rather agitated. Might you offer some insight?"

Bithia's ethereal voice rose above the noise. "My dears, I'm afraid they are these souls that I summoned when I was in body. They cling to this place."

Emboldened by Bithia's guidance, Nan addressed the

swirling spirits. "We wish to help you find peace. Please, tell us of your connection to this house, to Bithia."

The planchette moved once more, spelling out: "SECRETS. LIES. BETRAYAL."

Mabel gasped. "Nan, do you think... could this be about Bithia's death?"

Nan's mind raced, piecing together the fragments of family lore and ghostly whispers. "Bithia, your death... it wasn't an accident, was it?"

The room seemed to hold its breath, the spirits' swirling slowing to an anticipatory hover. Bithia's form flickered, a look of sorrow passing over her spectral features.

"No, my dear Nan," Bithia's voice echoed softly. "My demise," she began, her voice trembling like a fragile melody, "was far more... complicated than history would have you believe. I stayed to protect this house, but my presence has done little to soothe the pain woven into its walls."

As Bithia's words hung in the air a gust of wind swept through the room, extinguishing the candles and plunging the group into eerie darkness. The ornate furniture cast long, menacing shadows across the rich velvet upholstery. Nan's heart raced, her fingers trembling against the spirit board.

Abruptly, the malevolent presence filled the room, its dark energy palpable. The revenant that Bithia had warned them of had fully arrived.

"Cordelia!" Bithia's gut-wrenching cry filled the room. "Sister?"

Cordelia's spectral form materialized, her tattered lace gown billowing in an otherworldly breeze. Her hollow eyes burned with cold fury as she advanced on Nan and Mabel.

"Vanity and deceit!" Cordelia's voice hissed, dripping with bitter irony. "You dare speak of truth, sister?" Challenging eyes met Bithia's.

Bithia's protective aura flickered, struggling against

Cordelia's growing power. "Nan, my dear," Bithia called out, her voice strained, "you must stand firm!"

Nan's mind whirled. How could she possibly face this vengeful spirit? But as she gazed at Mabel's face, Nan found her center. She would not let this dark force harm her friend or taint her beloved home. She rolled her shoulders back and leveled her gaze, poised for victory.

"Now see here!" Nan declared, her voice carrying a hint of theatrical flair. "I'll not have you terrorizing my guests!" She placed her hands on her hips as she nudged a broken plate out of her way with the tip of her shoe. "This house is under my protection, and I intend to see all its spirits happy and free—yourself included, madam!"

Mabel squeezed Nan's hand. "We won't back down," she added, her sweet button nose scrunching with tenacity.

Cordelia's form swelled, her rage manifesting in a whirlwind that sent objects flying about the room. "You fool!" she shrieked. "You know nothing of the pain, the betrayal!"

Nan's pearl bracelet glinted as she gestured emphatically. "Then enlighten us, dear Cordelia! For I vow to rid this residence of your dark influence—by helping you find peace, if I must!"

As the battle of wills intensified, Nan silently prayed her Gemini-fueled adaptability would be enough to weather this supernatural storm.

As abruptly as it had begun, the cacophony ceased. The parlor fell into stillness; the only sound the ticking of the grandfather clock, its hands no longer spinning wildly. Nan's ears rang in the abrupt silence. The room remained in tatters.

"Goodness gracious," Nan breathed, her theatrical tone subdued. She turned to Mabel, whose wide eyes darted about the room. "I do believe a libation is in order, my dear."

Stepping over a pile of thrown books, Nan reached for the

crystal decanter on the nearby etagere. The bourbon sloshed precariously as she poured two generous glasses.

"Here we are," she said, passing one to Mabel. "A balm for rattled nerves, as my dear friend Bithia might say."

Mabel accepted the drink gratefully. "Nan, that was... extraordinary."

Nan sank into a velvet-upholstered chair, her sundress a cheerful contrast to her shaken demeanor. "Indeed."

As Mabel sipped her bourbon, Nan's thoughts drifted to Mossy. His gentle warnings echoed in her mind, a poetic refrain of caution she'd blithely ignored.

"Oh, Mossy," she murmured, more to herself than Mabel. "That man keeps me tethered when the winds of curiosity threaten to carry me away." She swirled her bourbon, the amber liquid catching the light. "But I wouldn't trade these flights of fancy—not for all the scientific caution in the world. Now, Mabel," she said, sitting taller, "let's see what else this house is hiding."

Mabel tilted her head, curiosity piqued. "Does Mossy often counsel against... supernatural pursuits?"

Nan chuckled softly. "My dear, that man has been trying to keep my feet firmly on the ground since the day we met. But you see," she whispered, leaning in conspiratorially, "I've always been rather fond of flying."

A Gentleman Makes His Exit

~~~

As the grandfather clock in the hallway chimed eleven, Nan smoothed the last dollop of night cream onto her cheeks with a contented sigh. Her cotton nightdress, adorned with delicate roses and forget-me-nots, rustled softly as she reached for Sir Arthur Conan Doyle's biography on her nightstand. A fabulous find in the downstairs library.

Beside her, Mossy settled into his pillow, his blue and white striped pajamas a lovely complement to the snuggly floral duvet. He poured water from the crystal decanter into the matching glass, the liquid gurgling melodiously in the quiet room.

"My word, Nan," Mossy breathed, his gaze drawn to the open window. "Would you look at that moon? It's positively resplendent above the old willow."

Nan glanced up from her book, a small smile playing on her lips. "Quite the romantic tonight, aren't we, dear?"

Mossy chuckled, the warm, rich sound filling the room. "Perhaps the spirits of Wordsworth and Shelley are afoot. Speaking of spirits," he continued while lifting his glasses to rub at his eye, "I've made remarkable progress on our plumbing conundrum."

Nan raised an eyebrow, her curiosity piqued despite herself. "Oh? Do tell, my love."

"Well," Mossy began, his hands painting invisible diagrams in the air, "it's all about the pressure, you see. I've devised a system of valves and pipes that will..."

As Mossy delved into the intricacies of his latest project, Nan found her thoughts drifting. She wondered what Sir Arthur would make of Bithia. Would he have attempted to commune with her through a séance? Or perhaps he'd have approached the matter with the same analytical mind that birthed Sherlock Holmes?

"...and that's when I realized," Mossy's animated voice broke through her reverie, "we could redirect the flow entirely!"

Nan blinked, quickly composing her features into an expression of rapt attention. "Fascinating, darling. Truly revolutionary."

As Mossy beamed with pride, Nan pondered the strange turns her life had taken. Here she was, mistress of a haunted bed and breakfast, married to a man who found plumbing as thrilling as she found the supernatural. And yet she wouldn't have it any other way.

A cool breeze rustled the curtains, carrying with it the faint scent of roses and sea salt. For a moment, Nan could have sworn she heard the whisper of silk skirts brushing against the floorboards. She shivered, not entirely from the chill.

"Mossy," she said softly, "do you ever wonder if Bithia approves of our renovations?"

Mossy paused mid-gesture. "My dear Nan, I'm certain Bithia is far more concerned with ethereal matters than the state of our plumbing."

Nan chuckled, her fingers absentmindedly tracing the embossed cover of her book. "Did you know," she mused, "that Sir Arthur Conan Doyle once attended a séance where the medium claimed to channel the spirit of his deceased son? Imagine that, Mossy! The creator of the world's most logical detective dabbling in the supernatural."

As Mossy resumed his animated explanation of valve configurations, Nan's gaze wandered around their bedroom. The faded damask wallpaper, once a vibrant peacock blue, now whispered of bygone eras in muted tones. Soft amber light from the bedside lamps cast a warm glow, creating dancing shadows that seemed to flirt with the possibility of spectral visitors.

Her eyes lingered on the ornate chifforobe in the corner, its intricate carvings of roses and vines almost lifelike in the flickering light. *I wonder*, Nan thought, *if Bithia ever kept her séance accoutrements hidden away in there.*

"Nan, my love?" Mossy's voice broke through her musings. "You seem rather distracted this evening. Perhaps we should call it a night?"

Nan smiled, reaching out to pat his hand affectionately. "Oh no, please continue. I'm finding your explanation of water pressure absolutely riveting. Almost as thrilling as the time Conan Doyle..." She trailed off, realizing she was about to embark on another tangent.

Nan's eyes drifted back to her book, fingers turning the delicate page. She attempted to focus on the page before her, but Mossy's words about pipe fittings and water pressure mingled with tales of Victorian spiritualism in her mind.

"Did you know," Nan interjected, her voice dreamy, "that Conan Doyle believed photographs could capture spirits? Imagine if our walls could speak. Or better yet, if they could show us what they've seen."

Nan's fingers brushed the embossed cover as a feeling of

familiarity overcame her. The pages fluttered though the windows were closed, and a cool draft swept across her cheeks. Her breath caught as the book began to tremble, then slowly rose from her hands as if guided by unseen fingers.

Nan's eyes widened, a gasp escaping her lips. Mossy, startled from his plumbing reverie, let out a yelp of surprise.

"Good heavens!" he exclaimed, his spectacles sliding down his nose. "Nan, my dear, I wish you would have agreed to leave that spirit board alone. These parlor tricks are hardly becoming of a respectable bed and breakfast proprietress— or of any rational person of this era."

Nan's laugh was breathy, almost a release of tension. "Oh, Mossy," she said, her voice softer than usual. "When faced with the ordinary or extraordinary, you at all times and in all ways are my gallant hero." A grin spread across her face. "Perhaps you'd care to employ your scientific reasoning to explain to our spectral friends that it's well past their bedtime? I'm sure they'd be quite impressed by your theories on water pressure and its application to the spirit world."

Mossy frowned, his brow furrowed. "Now, Nan, you know very well that—"

But before he could finish the book gently lowered itself back into Nan's waiting hands, as if accepting her playful admonishment. She stroked its cover lovingly, a conspiratorial smile playing on her lips.

"There, you see?" she said softly, more to the room than to Mossy. "Even ghosts can be reasoned with... though perhaps not always with science."

As if in response to Nan's gentle teasing, an eerie cacophony of sounds filled the room. The floorboards creaked with phantom footsteps, while the walls reverberated with muffled whispers and distant, echoing laughter. The sounds swelled and ebbed like an otherworldly tide, growing more insistent with each passing moment.

Mossy cleared his throat, his face a curious mixture of indignation and unease. "Now see here!" he proclaimed, puffing out his chest in a show of bravado, "I am the man of this house, and I demand that all this nonsense cease immediately!"

No sooner had the words left his lips than the ornate chandelier above their bed began to sway violently, its crystals tinkling a discordant melody. Nan felt her stomach lurch as the bed itself rose precariously into the air, hovering several inches above the floor.

"Good Lord!" Mossy exclaimed, his earlier bravado evaporating like mist. "There will be no more of these shenanigans, I say!"

Nan, her heart pounding like a hummingbird's wings, instinctively clutched Mossy's arm. "Oh my," she whispered as vertigo overtook her. "I don't believe Sir Arthur Conan Doyle ever wrote about anything quite like this!"

As quickly as it had begun, the supernatural maelstrom ceased. The bed gently settled back on the floor, the chandelier stilled, and an uncanny silence descended upon the room.

Mossy, his hair disheveled and his glasses askew, turned to Nan with a look of weary resignation. "My dear," he said, his voice quavering slightly, "perhaps it would be prudent if we were to... ah... relocate to the RV for the night. Just until we can ascertain the nature of these... disturbances."

Nan giggled despite the lingering tension in the air. "Oh, Mossy," she teased, patting his arm affectionately, "is the esteemed man of the house throwing in the towel so soon? And here I thought your scientific mind would be eager to observe this fascinating phenomenon!"

She sat up straighter, smoothing out her floral nightdress with a flourish. "No, my love, I shall stay right here. After all, what kind of hosts would we be if we abandoned our spectral guests at the first sign of tomfoolery?"

Mossy's frown deepened, etching lines of concern across his brow. With a heavy sigh that seemed to carry the weight of a thousand inexplicable encounters, he rose from the bed. His long, refined fingers fumbled with the knot of his robe's sash as he secured it over his pajamas.

"Very well, my dear," he said, his voice terse. "If you insist on staying, then I shall bid you goodnight. But know that you're welcome to join me in the RV at any time." He bent down, placing a gentle kiss on Nan's forehead. "Should the spirits prove too... spirited for your liking."

As Mossy gathered his pillow and book, Nan noticed how the moonlight caught his silver-white hair, giving him an almost spectral appearance of his own. "Oh, Mossy," she said, her countenance filled with mirth, "you do cut a dashing figure, even when retreating from phantoms."

Mossy paused, a wry smile playing at the corners of his mouth. "My darling Nan," he said, lingering in the doorway, "your wit could charm a banshee. But if the spirits toss you out of bed, do come join me in the RV. I've made up the bed— no levitating required." With that he slipped out of the room, his footsteps fading down the creaking stairs.

Left alone in the master bedroom, Nan felt her heart begin to race once more. The faded damask wallpaper seemed to pulse with an otherworldly energy, and shadows danced in the corners of her vision. Yet, as she gazed around the room, a curious sense of connection began to bloom within her chest.

"Well now," she whispered to the empty room, her voice carrying a hint of her old-world charm, "it seems we have some matters to discuss, don't we, my spectral friends?"

She took a deep breath, her fingers trembling slightly as she clutched her book tightly to her chest. The soft cotton of her floral nightdress rustled as she shifted in bed, the oversized pillow cradling her back.

"Sir Doyle," she said aloud, her voice carrying a theatrical lilt, "it's you and me now. I do hope you have some good ideas for me, old boy."

As if in response, the pages of the book fluttered and Nan let out a soft chuckle. "Oh, I see you're as eager as I am to get started."

She settled back against the pillows, opening the book to where she had left off. The soft glow of the bedside lamp cast a warm halo around her, creating a cozy island of light in the shadowy room.

"Now then," Nan murmured, her eyes scanning the pages, "let's see what insights you can offer on our current predicament."

As she read Nan found herself occasionally glancing up, her gaze darting around the room. The ornate chifforobe seemed to loom larger in the dimness, its carved details taking on an almost lifelike quality.

"I must say," she addressed the room at large, her voice soft as if speaking to a small child, "you spirits certainly know how to make an entrance. Perhaps you could go easy on old Mossy? He's a good old chap."

A gentle breeze rustled the lace curtains, carrying with it the faintest sound—like distant laughter, or the brush of silk against wood. Nan smiled, the earlier adrenalin replaced by a sense of hushed tranquility. "Well now," she whispered. "It seems we're in for quite the adventure, aren't we?"

She turned another page, her mind racing with possibilities.

"Oh, Sir Arthur," she whispered, "what a mystery we have on our hands. I do believe this calls for a proper investigation, don't you?"

As the night wore on Nan found herself utterly engrossed in her reading, occasionally jotting down notes on a pad she kept on her nightstand. The creaks and groans of the old house no longer startled her. Instead they seemed to harmonize with the rhythm of her thoughts, a symphony of the seen and unseen.

"Well," she said finally, stifling a yawn as she marked her place in the book, "I believe we've made a fine start." She ran her hand along Mossy's side of the bed. "Tomorrow, we shall continue our inquiries in earnest."

A Pixie Among the Petals

The knock at the door resounded with a pleasant, cheerful quality, as if the very wood had taken on a gleeful life of its own. Nan, ever the mistress of her domain, sprang from her task with the vigor of a woman half her age. "Mabel, do come in and make yourself at home!" she called from the kitchen, her voice lilting with the excitement of a child unwrapping a Christmas gift.

The door swung open, admitting a burst of sunlight that momentarily banished the entryway's warm, flickering shadows. Mabel stepped in, her large sun hat casting a dainty silhouette against the now-closed door. She paused, her bright eyes taking in the scene with the curiosity of a kitten. Following the sound of the ruckus, Mabel found herself in the kitchen. "Nan, sweetheart, whatever are you doing?" she inquired, a note of melodic concern threading her words.

For Nan had already thrust her head back into the cavernous maw of the oven, her favorite apron swaying like a pendulum. She withdrew slowly, a plume of flour in her hair giving her the aspect of a disheveled, yet cheerful, banshee. "I'm communing with the spirits of pastries past," she declared, waving a spatula with theatrical flourish. "Or perhaps just checking on the scones. One can never be too sure."

Mabel's laughter tinkled like wind chimes in a summer garden. "I feared you'd gone the way of poor Bithia, consigned to haunt your own kitchen."

"Not yet, my dearest Mabel," Nan replied, her eyes crinkling with a warmth that softened her teasing tone. "Though the way I burn through scones, it might be a fate worth considering. At least I'd haunt a kitchen full of good company."

Mabel placed a hand on Nan's arm, her voice dipping with affection. "Well, my dear, I'd gladly be your ghostly accomplice. Who else would keep you stocked in flowers and idle chatter?"

"Cleaning and organizing gives me quite the respite, my dear Mabel," Nan stated, her tone as light as whipped meringue. "The kitchen is the heart of this old house, after all." She wiped her hands down her checkered apron, the flour smudges blending into the fabric like ghostly fingerprints. "I made lemon curd to go with the rosewater scones."

Mabel's eyes widened with delight as she surveyed the room. An antique mahogany table dominated the center of the kitchen, acting as an island. Hanging above it was a full set of copper pots and pans, each gleaming with a well-loved patina. On the wall beneath a grand window that overlooked the front garden was a double-faucet sink, its porcelain chipped in places, telling the tale of many washings. Above the massive range hung an antique exhaust hood, angels engraved in the metal, their expressions a mixture of culinary rapture and divine duty.

"Oh, Nan, it's simply perfect," Mabel gushed, her voice a soft crescendo of admiration.

"Where is Mossy?" she inquired, her gaze lingering on the angelic exhaust hood.

Nan's smile took on a more contemplative curve. "We had a rather ghostly evening, and he's spent the day working in the back garden to clear his head."

With a flourish Mabel produced a bouquet of daffodils, their yellow trumpets bright as morning sun. "For you, my sweet. They symbolize new beginnings and friendship."

Nan graciously accepted the flowers. "They're beautiful, Mabel. Thank you." She pulled out an oversized vintage milk glass vase, its white surface opaline and soft to the eye. With the care of a florist and the affection of a friend, she began to arrange the flowers on the mahogany table.

"So," Mabel said, her tone turning ever so slightly conspiratorial, "what new beginnings are you planning, Nan?"

Nan paused, a daffodil in hand, and looked at her friend with a thoughtful gaze. "Oh, you know me, Mabel. I'm always ready for the next chapter, whatever it may be."

The two women stood in comfortable silence, the kind that only good friendships can sustain as the scent of lemon and daffodils mingled in the air.

As Nan admired the flowers, a sudden blur of yellow and green burst from the bouquet. A shock of yellow darted into the air, its gossamer wings a frantic blur. Both women leapt back, hands flying to their mouths in shock.

"Good heavens!" cried Nan. "A bee!"

Mabel's eyes widened as she grabbed a nearby tea towel, waving it with the fervor of a matador. "Shoo! Shoo!"

The form zigzagged through the air, narrowly avoiding Mabel's swipes and Nan's frantic hand-flapping.

"Begone, you stinging menace!" Nan shouted, ducking as the bee made a desperate swoop over her head.

What followed was a scene of pure bedlam; Nan and Mabel flailing and ducking, their makeshift weapons whirling through the air with the precision of a deranged windmill. The pint-sized menace zigzagged and loop-de-looped, its high-pitched protests drowned out by the women's shrieks and the slap of fabric on furniture.

The chaos reached a crescendo until Mabel, standing on tiptoe and waving the towel like a banner, abruptly froze. "Wait!" Mabel shouted, her tea towel freezing mid-air. Her eyes widened, narrowing in disbelief as the tiny figure hovered near the bouquet.

Nan blinked, still clutching her sandal like a shield. "What do you mean, wait? It's a bee!"

"Look closer," Mabel whispered, lowering the towel. The creature's wings slowed, catching the sunlight in a shimmering kaleidoscope of color. As it hovered lightly over the daffodils, Nan and Mabel leaned in, breathless with curiosity.

"Good heavens," Nan murmured, her voice trembling with awe. "It's... it's not a bee."

"No," Mabel confirmed, her voice tinged with wonder. "It's a pixie."

Nan froze mid-swat, her heeled sandal grasped tightly in hand. "A what?"

The pint-sized terror seized the moment, his wings slowing to a delicate flutter as he descended toward the table. He landed with a soft plink, standing beside the daffodils with a comically large pout. The women peered over, their expressions a mix of wonder and caution.

The pixie was about the size of a man's thumb, with a bald head, enormous eyes, and a sheepish smile that revealed a hint of impish pride. His red nose and long pointed ears gave him the appearance of a miniature elf, and his attire—leaves stitched together with spider silk—was both rustic and whimsical.

"A pixie," Nan repeated, her voice a mix of fascination and exasperation. "Well, that explains the glamour."

The pixie cleared his throat, the sound like the squeak of a mouse. "Ladies, I must protest," he declared, puffing out his chest as his wings gave an indignant flutter. "Such a reception is hardly befitting one of my stature. Pixie-kind demands a proper welcome—perhaps tea with honey next time?" He brushed an invisible speck from his leaf-stitched tunic. "Really, the decorum here is appalling." His voice was high and melodic, each word enunciated with the care of a courtier. "I am Bumbles, and I was quite content in Mabel's garden until you disturbed me."

Nan looked to Mabel, who shrugged with an apologetic smile. "I was only picking a few blooms for the breakfast table, in the name of friendship," she said.

"Indeed," Bumbles continued, his large eyes narrowing with feigned indignation. "Nan's garden is growing crowded with pixie factions, goblins and gnomes. I have observed your garden, dear lady, and it is in sore need of my expertise. I propose to take up residence and tend to it. In return, I shall make your flowers as enchanting as Mabel's."

Nan considered the pixie's offer, her mind racing with the possibilities. A garden tended by a pixie would indeed be a marvel, but the thought of adding yet another supernatural element to the bed and breakfast gave her pause.

"Spirits and pixies," she mused aloud, her eyes drifting to the skeleton key that hung around her neck. "It might all be too much for one B&B."

Bumbles' wings drooped, and for a moment he looked like a dejected child. "I assure you, I am no trouble. The flowers will speak of my skill, and your guests will be most delighted."

Nan sighed, her kind heart already yielding. "Very well, Bumbles. You may stay—for now. But remember, this is a place for guests. We mustn't overwhelm them with too much enchantment."

The pixie's face lit up with a radiant smile, his eyes sparkling with newfound playfulness. "You shall not regret it. Your garden will be the talk of the town."

With that Bumbles took to the air, his wings a blur of gossamer as he circled the room in a joyful arc. Nan and Mabel watched him, their expressions filled with amusement.

"Well," said Mabel, her voice lilting with its usual optimism. "At least we'll both have the most magical flowers in all of Daytona."

Nan could only nod, her thoughts already turning to the next whimsical challenge that Nettles' B&B would undoubtedly face.

Bumbles hovered in the air, his wings creating a soft, persistent hum. "What do you mean about spirits?" he asked, tilting his head with curious intent.

Nan exchanged a glance with Mabel, who gave a small, encouraging nod. "You see, Bumbles," Nan began, her voice taking on the cadence of a storyteller, "we are turning this delightful abode into a bed and breakfast. But, alas, it has a long, storied history. It was once the home of Bithia, a renowned spiritualist who held séances here. Even now, her spirit lingers."

Mabel chimed in, her tone as bright as the sunflowers that adorned her sundress. "Bithia is a friendly ghost, of course. We're quite fond of her."

Bumbles' large eyes grew even rounder. "Ah, a house with a ghostly patron! How delightful— and that you are both believers!"

"It's not a matter of belief," Nan said, her fingers lightly touching the key around her neck. "It's a matter of experience. During the renovations, we've had our fair share of... unexplainable events. Unfortunately, not all were pleasant. We have found to our great worry that there is, within the residence, a revenant!"

The pixie bobbed in the air thoughtfully. "I see. So, your concern is that another layer of enchantment might upset the balance."

"Exactly," said Nan.

Bumbles landed delicately on the edge of a teacup, his tiny hands clasped in a gesture of earnestness. "I understand your apprehension. But know this: I have lived among humans for many years, and I have a keen understanding of the supernatural. Spirits, like the one you describe, are not so different from us pixies. They have desires, fears, and a need for recognition."

Nan raised an eyebrow, intrigued despite herself. "And you think you can handle them?"

"I can command respect among my own kind," Bumbles said, a note of pride creeping into his high-pitched voice. "And I have a few tricks up my sleeve when it comes to dealing with otherworldly beings. My presence here could be more of an asset than you realize."

Mabel's eyes shimmered with the possibilities. "Imagine, Nan, a garden so enchanting that it draws in more guests. And with Bumbles' help, we could ensure that everything remains in harmony."

Nan sighed. "It's not that I doubt your abilities, Bumbles. It's just... this house, this garden—is already so much to manage. Ghosts, renovations, future guests... sometimes I worry that I'm losing sight of what will make this place feel like home."

Bumbles hovered closer, his wings humming softly. "And what is home, Lady Nan, if not a place where the extraordinary feels ordinary? I promise my magic will add harmony, not chaos."

Silence settled over the room, broken only by the distant sound of Mossy working in the back yard.

"Very well," Nan said at last. "We'll give it a try."

Bumbles' face lit up with a mischievous grin. "You shall not regret it. The Nettles' B&B will be the most enchanted place in all the land."

With that the pixie took to the air once more, his wings a blur as he again made a joyful circuit of the room. Nan and Mabel watched him, wondering what new chapter had just begun.

Nan, Mabel, and Bumbles convened in the parlor, where the soft glow of gaslight and the scent of aged mahogany created an ambiance of timelessness. The tiny pixie hovered above a porcelain teacup as he surveyed the two women.

"The disturbances have grown more frequent," Nan observed, her voice tinged with the kind of concern a matron might have for a wayward child. "Last night, there was quite a spectacle in the bedroom."

Bumbles voice cut through the tension. "The enchantment that surrounds this place is delicate. Without proper guardianship, it is vulnerable to all manner of supernatural intrusions."

Nan turned to the pixie, her eyes softening. "I am most grateful for your offer to help, Bumbles."

Mabel's face lit up with the warmth of a summer sunrise. "It would be like having a guardian angel—albeit a very small one."

Bumbles puffed out his tiny chest, his wings fluttering with an air of authority. "The pixies have long been the guardians of balance and tradition," he declared before nearly toppling backward onto a teacup. "And though my stature is modest, my skills are unparalleled—though perhaps I should keep both feet firmly on the ground for now."

Nan hesitated for a moment, her thoughts flickering like a candle flame. "It's a generous offer, Bumbles. We know that your kind thrives in the wild, not in human gardens."

The pixie's large, expressive eyes met Nan's, and for a moment the mischievous sparkle in them was replaced by something deeper, almost solemn. "The wild is where we find our joy, it's true. But we also find joy in places where magic is alive. Your garden is such a place."

"Very well," Nan said at last, her voice as gentle as a mother's lullaby. "Let me show you the garden. We will do everything we can to make it hospitable for you and your kin."

With that, the pixie took to the air. Nan carefully arranged an assortment of delicacies on a shiny silver tea tray.

With Nan leading the way, carrying a tray of pastries and tea, Bumbles and Mabel meandered through the winding paths of the yard towards the rose garden. They walked in silence, taking in the beauty around them.

As they approached the entrance of the rose garden, Bumbles let out a high-pitched squeal that echoed through the air. To Nan and Mabel's amazement, tiny figures began to appear in front of them. They were surrounded by a swarm of colorful pixies, each no bigger than a ladybug.

Nan and Mabel gasped in unison as the air came alive with the fluttering of delicate wings, their surfaces catching the sunlight like shards of rainbow glass. The soft, tinkling laughter of the pixies blended with the rustle of leaves, creating a melody as light and fleeting as the summer breeze. The heady scent of blooming roses mingled with the earthy aroma of damp soil, wrapping them in an otherworldly embrace.

Bumbles flew up to one of his fellow pixies and spoke to them in their melodic language. The other pixie nodded and flew off, disappearing into a cluster of roses.

"What is happening?" Mabel whispered in awe.

"We are being welcomed," Bumbles replied, a proud twinkle in his eye.

Nan smiled, her heart warmed by this display of friendship from the pixies. She led them further into the garden, where a white iron table with cushy chairs was set up underneath a magnificent arbor covered in purple blooms.

"This looks like it came straight out of a fairytale," Mabel exclaimed as she took her seat.

Nan chuckled. "It certainly feels that way." She set down the tea tray and poured tea from a luxurious porcelain teapot into delicate teacups while Mabel spread lemon curd onto rosewater scones. The scent of roses and freshly brewed tea filled their senses as they indulged in their treats.

"This lemon curd is divine," Mabel said with a contented sigh.

"It goes perfectly with these rosewater scones," Nan agreed.

As they chatted and enjoyed their teatime amongst their new pixie friends Nan and Mabel exchanged a glance, their smiles brimming with amusement as Bumbles directed a chorus of pixies to tidy the garden.

"Well," Mabel said, taking another sip of tea, "I suppose we've officially entered a fairytale."

Nan chuckled, tilting her head toward the distant house. "If only Mossy could see this. I'm sure he'd have a practical suggestion for pixie management."

As Bumbles darted over to supervise a particularly unruly gnome statue, his tiny voice rang out. "Ladies, the garden is just the beginning. Wait until you see what I have planned next!"

Nan smiled. Whatever enchantments lay ahead, she was ready.

The Hidden Door

The delicate porcelain teacup clinked softly as Nan set it upon its saucer, her brow furrowed in contemplation. The fragrant aroma of Earl Grey mingled with the sweet perfume of roses created an enchanting bouquet that drifted lazily through the garden air. They had spent several hours working over the garden at Bumbles' behest, and now were enjoying a much-deserved respite.

"I must confess, dearest Mabel," Nan began, her voice tinged with a theatrical sigh, "our efforts to unravel the enigma of Bithia's past have been rather... unfruitful."

Mabel tilted her sun hat, the oversized brim casting her freckled face into shadow. "Indeed, my dear Nan. It's as if we're trying to catch moonbeams with a butterfly net!"

Nan chuckled, the laughter softening her brow. "Oh, Mabel, you do have a way with words. But I fear these strange occurrences in the house are becoming more frequent. Just yesterday, I found all the sugar cubes stacked in a perfect pyramid. And I'm quite certain I didn't do it."

As Mabel opened her mouth to respond, a glint of light

caught Nan's eye. She turned, her gaze drawn upward to the highest reaches of Nettles' B&B. There, nestled among the gables and weathered shingles, a single window stood out from its fellows, faintly aglow.

"Mabel," Nan whispered, her voice barely audible over the gentle rustle of rose petals, "do you see that?"

Mabel followed Nan's gaze, her eyes widening behind her oversized sunglasses. "Oh my! That window... it's positively aglow!"

Indeed, the window appeared slightly ajar, a faint, otherworldly light spilling forth from within.

"I don't recall ever noticing that window before," Nan mused. "Do you suppose it could be... Bithia?"

Mabel leaned forward, her eyes filled with curiosity. "Oh, wouldn't that be splendid? Perhaps she's trying to guide us, like a spectral lighthouse keeper!"

Nan smiled at her friend's enthusiasm even as her own heart raced. "Well, my dear Mabel, it seems our afternoon tea has taken a rather supernatural turn. Shall we investigate this luminous mystery?"

As they rose from their seats, teacups abandoned in favor of adventure, Nan couldn't shake the feeling that they were on the precipice of uncovering something extraordinary. The key around her neck seemed to pulse with an otherworldly warmth, as if responding to the siren call of that curious, glowing window.

Mabel clapped her hands with delight, her garden apron fluttering in the breeze. "Oh, Nan! What an adventure this shall be! Perhaps we'll uncover the secret to Bithia's enchanting séances."

As they turned to make their way back into the house, a faint buzzing filled the air. Bumbles appeared before them, his tiny form shimmering with its customary iridescent glow. His wings beat furiously as he hovered at eye level, his high-pitched voice tinged with concern.

"Dearest ladies, we humbly request to join your expedition," Bumbles declared, his formal tone at odds with his diminutive size. "The spirits are restless this day, and we pixies offer our protection."

Nan raised an eyebrow, her lips quirking into an amused smile. "Protection, you say? And here I thought you lot were more inclined towards puckishness than guardianship."

Bumbles puffed out his tiny chest. "I assure you, Madame Nettles, we are most capable in matters of the supernatural."

Mabel giggled, her eyes dancing with mirth. "Oh, do let them come, Nan! They're ever so delightful, and who knows what their pixie magic might reveal?"

Nan sighed dramatically though her eyes twinkled with humor. "Very well, but mind you don't go rearranging the furniture while we're up there. I've only just got the parlor and the kitchen sorted."

As they made their way towards the house, the key around her neck seemed to grow heavier with each step.

The grand foyer stretched before them, its newly polished mahogany stairs gleaming in the soft light of crystal chandeliers. Nan led the way, her hand gliding along the smooth banister as they ascended.

"I do hope we're not disturbing any ghostly teatimes," Mabel whispered, her voice tinged with enthusiasm.

Nan chuckled softly. "My dear, I believe our spectral residents prefer the witching hour for their soirées."

As they reached the second floor Bumbles zipped past them. "This way, ladies! The attic beckons with its secrets!"

The group proceeded in single file, their footsteps muffled by the plush carpet. Nan marveled at the juxtaposition of the immaculate lower floors and the musty, cobweb-draped staircase that led to the attic. Stacks of yellowing newspapers and leather-bound tomes lined the narrow passage, creating a literary gauntlet.

"Oh my," Mabel exclaimed, brushing a cobweb from her hair. "I daresay we've stumbled into a rather Gothic scene, haven't we?"

Nan nodded, her eyes scanning the shadowy recesses. "Indeed. One might almost expect to find Mr. Rochester's wife lurking in these corners."

As they entered the attic proper, a collective gasp escaped their lips. The vast space was a veritable treasure trove of antiques, each item whispering tales of bygone eras.

Bumbles and his pixie cohorts darted about, their ethereal glow illuminating dusty curios and forgotten heirlooms. "Look here!" he chirped, hovering near a tarnished music box. "Such wonders!"

A chill swept through the room, causing goosebumps to rise on Nan's arms. She shivered, her voice barely above a whisper. "Did you feel that, Mabel?"

Mabel nodded, her eyes wide. "Like a ghostly caress. And listen... do you hear those whispers?"

Indeed, faint murmurs seemed to float on the air, just beyond comprehension. Nan strained her ears, trying to decipher the spectral conversation.

Bumbles flitted back to them, his usual mischievous demeanor replaced by an air of gravity. "Miladies," he said, his tiny voice solemn, "I must inform you of a most curious discovery. Behind yonder mirror," he intoned, gesturing to an enormous, gilt-framed looking- glass, "lies a hidden door."

Nan's hand instinctively went to the key hanging around her neck. "A hidden door?" she mused, her heart quickening. "Well, Mabel, it seems our little excursion has taken quite the turn. Shall we see what lies beyond?"

Mabel nodded enthusiastically, her sun hat bobbing and her sunglasses in hand. "Oh, absolutely! Let's unearth this mystery, petal by petal."

With a decisive nod, Nan addressed the pixies. "Right then, my little luminaries. Help us clear a path to that mirror, if you please."

The pixies darted about, illuminating forgotten treasures as they worked. Nan and Mabel joined in, carefully moving aside dusty tomes and antiquated bric-a-brac.

"I do hope we're not disturbing any ghostly tenants," Mabel quipped, setting aside a particularly garish porcelain figurine.

Nan chuckled, her hands fluttering as she delicately moved the relics out of the way.

Finally, they stood before the ornate mirror. Nan's reflection stared back at her, silver and brown curls slightly askew, eyes wide with wonder. She placed her hand on the cool glass, surprised to feel it give way slightly.

"Mabel, darling, would you assist me?" Nan asked, her voice trembling with excitement.

Together, they pushed the mirror aside, revealing a weathered wooden door. An old-fashioned keyhole winked at them, as if daring them to unlock its secrets.

Mabel gasped. "Nan! Your key—the one around your neck. Do you suppose...?"

Nan's fingers instinctively went to the chain. "Why, it's worth a try, isn't it?"

With trembling hands, Nan removed the key and inserted it into the lock. A moment of breathless expectancy, and then — click! The door swung open with a creak that seemed to echo through time itself.

As they stepped into the hidden room, Nan's heart raced. What secrets lay within? What whispers of the past awaited their discovery? The dust motes danced in the air, lending an air of enchantment to the moment.

"Oh my," Nan breathed, her eyes wide as she took in the scene before her. "Mabel, I do believe we've stumbled upon something truly extraordinary."

Nan took in the hidden room, her heart fluttering like a caged bird. Antique furniture loomed in the shadows, their ornate curves hinting at forgotten elegance. Faded photographs adorned the walls, faces from the past staring out with haunting intensity.

"Good heavens!" Mabel exclaimed. "Nan, look at this marvelous contraption!"

Nan turned to see Mabel hovering over an ancient gramophone, its brass horn gleaming dully in the pixies' ethereal light. Beside it lay a collection of dusty records, their handwritten labels promising glimpses into Bithia's mysterious séances.

"Shall we..." Nan began, her voice catching. "Shall we listen to one?"

Mabel nodded eagerly, carefully placing a record on the turntable. As the needle touched down, Nan held her breath, half-expecting only the crackle of static. Instead, a voice emerged—cultured, refined, and unmistakably Bithia's.

"Tonight, we seek to pierce the veil," the recording intoned. "Join hands, dear friends, and open your minds to the beyond."

The pixies, as if compelled by some unseen force, began to swirl and coalesce. Their collective glow formed ghostly outlines: Bithia and four others, hands clasped around a table. Nan watched transfixed as the ethereal scene unfolded before her.

A bone-chilling voice cut through the air, causing Nan to clutch Mabel's arm instinctively. "I am here," it rasped, "and I hunger."

Bithia's voice, now trembling with fear, came through the gramophone. "Who... who are you? What do you want? Cordelia!"

The recording ended abruptly, plunging the room into eerie silence.

"Goodness," Mabel whispered, her usual cheerfulness subdued. "That was rather unsettling, wasn't it?"

Nan nodded, her mind racing. "Indeed." She took a moment to compose herself. "But look here, Mabel! A journal!"

With trembling fingers, Nan picked up the worn leather-bound book. Opening it carefully, she began to read aloud:

"April 15th, 1924. Excitement abounds! The great Houdini himself has agreed to attend one of my séances. Oh, how I long to prove the authenticity of my gifts to such a renowned skeptic!"

She paused, her brow furrowed. "But listen to this next part, Mabel. 'Cordelia grows colder by the day. Her eyes, once so full of sisterly affection, now burn with... something else. Jealousy? Or perhaps... no, I mustn't entertain such thoughts.'"

As Nan read, the pixies once again began to move, creating a shimmering tableau. Two women, unmistakably Bithia and Cordelia, stood facing each other. The tension between them was palpable even in this ghostly reenactment.

"There's more," Nan continued, her voice hushed. "Last night's séance... something came through. Something dark, malevolent. I haven't felt myself since. It's as if a shadow has fallen over my very soul. And yet, it is Cordelia I fear for. Her mood and mannerisms have been most foul."

Mabel shuddered. "Gracious, Nan. What on earth happened to poor Bithia and Cordelia?"

Nan closed the journal slowly, her fingers lingering on the worn leather as if the weight of Bithia's secrets had transferred to her own heart. "Oh, Mabel," she murmured, her voice trembling, "whatever happened between the sisters wasn't just tragic—it was catastrophic. I can feel it in these pages."

Mabel's hands trembled as she reached for a stack of sepia-toned photographs, her eyes widening as she recognized the subjects. "Oh, Nan," she breathed, "look at these. It's Bithia and Cordelia, in their younger years."

Nan leaned in, her eyes scanning the images. Two young women, their faces alight with laughter, stood arm in arm in a sun-dappled garden. "They look so happy," Nan murmured, her heart aching for the sisterly bond that had clearly soured.

A bone-chilling wind gusted through the room. The pixies, previously fluttering about in curious exploration, now swarmed in a frenzied mass, their tiny bodies glowing with an otherworldly magic.

"Goodness gracious!" Mabel exclaimed, clutching Nan's arm. "What on earth is happening?"

As if in answer, the pixies began to coalesce, forming two distinct, ghostly figures. Nan watched as the reenactment of the fateful event unfolded before her. Two girls, unmistakably Bithia and Cordelia, stood by the window. In a horrifying instant, one figure shoved the other, sending her tumbling out into the night.

"Oh, Bithia," Nan whispered, her voice catching. "What happened to you?"

Taking a deep breath Nan called out, her voice quavering slightly, "Bithia? Bithia, are you here?"

A shimmering form materialized before them, the ghostly visage of Bithia Mary Croker regarding them with a sad demeanor.

"Bithia," Nan began, her heart pounding, "is it... is it possible that Cordelia... pushed you out the window?"

Bithia's spectral form wavered, her eyes filled with pain. "My dear Nan," she replied, her voice echoing with the formal cadence of a bygone era, "if Cordelia did indeed commit such a heinous act, I assure you it was not of her own free will."

As if summoned by Bithia's words another icy gust tore through the room, scattering antiques and sending papers flying. Nan and Mabel huddled together, fear etched on their faces.

"Oh, my word," Mabel whimpered, "I do believe I've had quite enough of ghostly encounters for one day!"

Mabel and Nan were pushed closer to the window by the strong gusts of wind, until the panes of glass abruptly flew open with such violent force the glass shattered. "Oh my goodness, we're going to be tossed out!" Nan exclaimed in panic.

The pixies, sensing the women's distress, quickly formed a protective forcefield around them, their tiny bodies humming with energy. As the wind subsided, Nan and Mabel felt a sense of relief wash over them. They were finally able to stand firm and move away from the window.

Nan's mind raced, trying to piece together the fragments of information they'd uncovered. "Bithia," she asked, her voice steadier now, "what do you mean, 'not of her own free will'? Was Cordelia... possessed?"

Nan noticed the sadness reflected in Bithia's eyes, making her wonder if they had unintentionally discovered a horrifying truth.

With trembling hands, Nan reached for the worn journal and scattered photographs. The room, once filled with spectral energy, now felt eerily still, as if holding its breath.

"We must take these downstairs," Nan whispered, her voice barely audible over the gentle hum of the pixies' protective field. "There's more to this mystery than meets the eye, Mabel dear."

Mabel nodded, her usually rosy cheeks pale with shock. "Indeed," she replied, her voice quavering. "Though I must say,

I never thought I'd be embroiled in a Victorian ghost story outside of my beloved penny dreadfuls!"

As they gathered the items, Nan's mind whirled with possibilities. What dark force could have compelled Cordelia to harm her own sister? And why did Bithia seem so accepting of it all?

"One does wonder," Nan mused aloud, "if we're not opening a Pandora's box of sorts. Though I suppose it's a bit late to stuff the spirits back in, isn't it?"

Mabel let out a nervous titter. "Dear me."

With their precious cargo secured, they made their way to the door. Nan paused, fishing the ornate key from around her neck. As she turned the key a wave of melancholy washed over her, accompanied by the faintest echo of a sigh—soft, forlorn, and unmistakably not her own. She glanced at Mabel, who seemed oblivious, and decided to keep the moment to herself for now.

"Bithia," she called softly, "we'll get to the bottom of this, I promise."

The air shimmered, and Bithia's ghostly form appeared once more. Her eyes, filled with otherworldly wisdom, locked onto Nan's.

"My dear, brave Nan," Bithia whispered, her voice carrying the weight of decades, "your willingness to uncover the truth... it means more than you can possibly know. Be cautious, for the past often holds dangers we cannot foresee."

As Bithia faded away, Nan felt a chill. What secrets lay hidden in the pages of that journal? And, more importantly, were they truly prepared for what they might find?

The mahogany stairs creaked beneath their feet as Nan, Mabel, and their pixie entourage descended from the attic. Shafts of late afternoon sunlight filtered through the crystal chandelier, casting prismatic rainbows across the faded wallpaper. Nan clutched the worn journal to her chest, its musty scent mingling with the ever-present aroma of sea salt and jasmine that permeated her abode.

Mabel, her sun hat slightly askew from their attic adventure, turned to Nan with wide eyes. "Darling, I feel as though we've stumbled into one of Bithia's séances ourselves!"

The pixies, glowing like fireflies in the dimming light, swirled around them in agitation. Bumbles, ever the dramatic one, mimed fainting onto Mabel's hat.

"Now, now," Mabel cooed, gently shooing the pixie off her brim, "let's not get ahead of ourselves. Remember, every flower must push through the dirt before it can bloom."

Nan smiled at her friend's whimsical wisdom. "You're right, of course. But I can't shake the feeling that we're on the precipice of something... monumental." She paused on the landing, her fingers tracing the embossed cover of Bithia's journal. "What if... what if Cordelia truly did push Bithia? The implications are simply ghastly!"

As they continued their descent, Nan's mind raced. Could sibling rivalry have led to such a tragic end? Or was there something more sinister at play?

"You know," Mabel mused, interrupting Nan's reverie, "my gran always said that secrets were like weeds— the deeper the roots, the harder they are to pull out."

Nan chuckled softly, grateful for her friend's grounding presence. "Your gran was a wise woman, Mabel. I just hope we're prepared for whatever we might uncover."

As they reached the bottom of the stairs, the warm glow of the setting sun bathed the foyer in golden light. Nan took a deep breath, steeling herself for the task ahead.

"Well, my dear," she said, turning to Mabel with a glint in her eye, "shall we brew another pot of Earl Grey and dive into this mystery? I have a feeling we're in for quite the spectral soirée." She glanced over toward the kitchen, "I'm going to put dinner in the oven. Roast chicken and all the trimmings should cheer Mr. Nettles after his long day of yard work."

Mabel nodded enthusiastically, already heading towards the kitchen. "I'll handle the tea," Mabel chirped, already donning an apron. "Something tells me we'll need more than just courage to untangle this web of spectral intrigue—perhaps an extra dash of sugar as well. And Nan, do add a little extra rosemary to that chicken; even ghosts deserve a fragrant meal."

A Romance Under the Stars

~~~

The candlelight flickered, casting soft, fluid shadows across the dining room. The scent of beeswax and roasted thyme mingled in the air as Nan and Mossy savored the final bites of their meal, the faint strains of *La Traviata* mingling with the gentle clink of silverware against Wedgwood china.

Nan's flowing blue dress shimmered in the soft light, her pearls capturing the warm glow of the candlelight. She watched with amusement as Mossy, looking dapper in his crisp white shirt, self-consciously brushed his damp hair from his forehead for the umpteenth time that evening.

"My dear Mrs. Nettles," Mossy began, his voice warm with admiration, "you've turned roasted chicken into art."

Nan's eyes twinkled with delight. "Why, Mr. Nettles, you flatter me so. One might think you were trying to charm your way into seconds."

Mossy chuckled, his eyes crinkling behind his thin spectacles. "Charm has nothing to do with it, my love. Your culinary prowess speaks for itself." He paused, choosing his next words with the care of a poet. "You've transformed our daily sustenance into an art form, a nightly celebration of life's simple pleasures."

Nan felt a warmth bloom in her cheeks, touched by her husband's heartfelt words. She reached across the table, her fingers intertwining with his. "And you, my dear, have elevated our dinner conversations to the realm of poetry. I daresay even our spectral houseguest might be envious of our repartee."

Mossy's eyebrows shot up, a mix of amusement and exasperation crossing his face. "Ah, yes, our ethereal lodger. I do hope she's not eavesdropping on our private moments."

Nan laughed, the sound echoing through the cozy room. "Now, now, darling. I'm sure Bithia has better things to do than listen to our idle chatter."

Mossy shook his head, a fond smile playing on his lips. "Only you, my dear, could make ghost-hunting sound like a perfectly ordinary pastime." He lifted his glass, proposing a toast. "To us, and to the extraordinary life we've built in this wonderfully peculiar home of ours."

As their glasses clinked Nan felt a surge of gratitude for the man before her, who indulged her flights of fancy with such grace. "Speaking of our extraordinary life," she said, her voice taking on a conspiratorial tone, "you'll never guess what Mabel and I discovered in the attic today."

Mossy leaned forward, his interest piqued despite his usual skepticism. "Do tell, my dear. What mystical wonders have you unearthed now?"

Nan's words tumbled out in a breathless rush. "Oh, Mossy, it was absolutely thrilling! Mabel and I were rummaging through the dusty old attic this afternoon, when we stumbled upon a door hidden behind a large mirror. Can you believe it? A secret room!"

She paused, absently twirling her pearls as she savored the memory. "And inside... oh, inside was a treasure trove of Bithia's belongings. Journals, a gramophone, and old recordings of Bithia's seances. It was like stepping into a Victorian spiritualist's parlor."

Mossy furrowed his brow in consternation, his fingers tapping a restless rhythm on the tablecloth. "My dear, while I admire your enthusiasm, I can't help but wonder if we're letting our imaginations run a tad wild. Perhaps it was simply a storage space, long forgotten."

Nan shook her head, undeterred. "No, no, you should have seen it. There were photographs, Mossy. Photographs of Bithia with the Rockefellers! And her journals... they speak of such extraordinary phenomena. I truly believe we're on the brink of unraveling a great mystery."

As Nan continued her animated recounting, Mossy's gaze drifted to the bookshelf across the room. His eyes lingered on the leather-bound volumes of Tennyson and Wordsworth, seeking comfort in their familiar spines.

"My love," he said softly, interrupting Nan's flow of words as he stood and walked to the bookcase, "while I find your tales intriguing, I confess I struggle to reconcile them with the world as I understand it." He reached for a nearby book, his fingers caressing its worn cover. "Perhaps we might spend the evening with some poetry instead? I've been longing to revisit Keats' "Ode on a Grecian Urn"."

Nan's eyes softened, a mix of affection and amusement dancing in their depths. She sauntered over to Mossy, reliving him of his book and laced her fingers with his. "Oh, my dear, always seeking solace in your beloved verses," she said, her voice warm with fondness. "But tell me, have you never yearned for a touch of the extraordinary?"

Mossy's gaze drifting to the flickering candlelight. "Well," he began, his voice taking on a dreamy quality, "I suppose if I were to entertain the notion of spectral companions, I'd rather fancy one like Sir Simon from Wilde's *The Canterville Ghost*.

A charming fellow, wouldn't you agree? Adding a dash of whimsy to our daily routines."

Nan's laughter bubbled up, light and melodious. "Ah, but don't you remember, my love? Sir Simon was quite terrified of the American family that moved into Canterville Chase. Perhaps it's not us who should fear the spirits, but they who fear us!"

Mossy raised an eyebrow, a smile tugging at the corners of his mouth. "An intriguing perspective, my dear. Though I must admit, the thought of frightening a ghost seems rather... well, ghastly."

"Oh, pish posh." Nan waved her hand dismissively. "I'm certain we have nothing to fear from our dear Bithia. After all, she's been here all along, hasn't she? Watching over this house, perhaps even guiding us to it."

Mossy leaned back in his chair, considering. "I suppose when you put it that way, it does sound rather... enchanting. Like something out of one of your beloved Victorian novels."

"Exactly!" Nan exclaimed as she guided Mossy back to the dining table and took her seat. "Just think, darling. We could be living our very own supernatural romance. Isn't that far more exciting than another evening with Keats?"

Mossy's expression clouded, eyes turning stormy as he traced the outline of his fork with a gentle touch. "My dearest Nan, while I admire your enthusiasm for the ethereal I must confess that last night's... incident has left me rather unsettled." He paused, brushing a wayward lock of hair from his forehead. "Our bed levitating was hardly the stuff of whimsical poetry. I fear I cannot shake the desire for a touch of normalcy, a dash of the practical."

Nan frowned, her fingers absently toying with her pearl necklace. "Darling, surely you don't mean—"

"I do," Mossy interrupted, his voice soft but resolute. "Until we've unraveled this supernatural conundrum, I believe it prudent to seek refuge in the RV. A temporary measure, you understand, to preserve my sanity and, dare I say, our safety."

A coy smile played on Nan's lips. She rose gracefully, her dress swirling around her ankles as she glided to Mossy's side. "Oh, my dear Mr. Nettles," she purred while leaning over him, her hand leisurely trailing up his leg, "must you be so dreadfully rational?"

Mossy's breath caught as Nan's fingers danced along his thigh. "I... well, that is to say..."

"Come now," Nan whispered, leaning close, her pearls catching the candlelight. "Surely you don't need spectral assistance to make our bed... tremble?" She winked. "What say we retire upstairs and conduct our own séance of sorts? I assure you, no spirits required."

Mossy's gaze drifted to the key dangling from Nan's neck, its antique brass glinting in the candlelight. He cleared his throat, a mixture of desire and yearning coloring his voice. "My dear, er... do you suppose our spectral tenant might grant us a modicum of privacy this evening?"

With deliberate slowness Nan lifted the chain from around her neck, the key swaying gently as she placed it on the table with a soft clink. "Bithia, darling?" she called out to the empty room, her voice honeyed with playful intent. "Mr. Nettles requires my undivided attention for the remainder of the night. Be a dear and give us some privacy, won't you?"

A sudden breeze rustled the lace curtains, and Mossy could have sworn he heard a faint, ghostly chuckle. He swallowed hard, his poet's heart racing with a rhythm far more primal than iambic pentameter.

Rising from his chair Mossy grasped Nan's hand, helping her to her feet. As she stood he pulled her close, their bodies fitting together like two halves of a long-lost locket. His voice dropped to a husky whisper as he quoted:

"'She walks in beauty, like the night
Of cloudless climes and starry skies;
And all that's best of dark and bright
Meet in her aspect and her eyes...'"

Nan's breath caught as Mossy's arms encircled her waist. "Byron, my love? How deliciously scandalous."

Mossy's eyes, usually as calm as a misty moor, now smoldered with barely contained passion. "You inspire poetry in my very soul, my dear. Shall we... continue this discussion upstairs?"

With desire in her eyes Nan pressed a finger to Mossy's lips, halting his poetic flow. "Oh, my darling Byron," she teased, her laughter like tinkling bells.

Mossy felt a delightful shiver run through him. His scholarly mind, usually lost in dusty tomes and ethereal verses, was hyper-aware of Nan's warmth; her scent, the way her chest heaved with anticipating breath. He was utterly bewitched, not by any supernatural force but by the very real, very enchanting woman before him.

With a flourish that would have made Sir Simon de Canterville proud, Mossy leaned over the table and blew out the candles. The dining room was plunged into a soft, intimate darkness, broken only by slivers of moonlight sneaking through the curtains.

"Follow me, Mrs. Nettles," Mossy said, his voice low and filled with passion. He grasped Nan's hand, delighted at how perfectly it fit in his own. "I believe we have some magic of our own to conjure."

Nan's laughter, rich and full of joy, echoed through the house as Mossy led her towards the stairs. It bounced off the walls, filling every nook and cranny of their beloved abode with the sound of pure, mortal happiness.

As they ascended Mossy marveled at the woman beside

him, her laughter ringing like music through their home. Ghosts and mysteries might surround them, but here, in her touch and her smile, was the truest magic he had ever known.

Whispers from the Past

Golden sunlight filtered through the parted velvet drapes, pooling on the parlor's polished wood floors and gilding the room in warmth. Nan perched on the edge of a high-backed chair, her ivory sweater a bright contrast to the rich burgundy upholstery. The pearls at her neck glinted faintly as she traced their cool surface with restless fingers. Her gaze lingered on the bouquet of black calla lilies in the silver vase before her, their dark elegance a striking counterpoint to the morning's golden hues. But her thoughts were far from flowers. Somewhere in this house was the missing key, and its absence gnawed at her like a loose thread in an otherwise perfect tapestry.

"Darling, I must say, your Eggs Benedict were simply divine," Mabel declared, her deep purple sundress rustling as she leaned forward to set down her crystal flute. "I don't believe I've ever tasted better."

Nan managed a wan smile, her usual effervescence dimmed by worry. "Thank you, dear. I'm glad you enjoyed them. But I'm afraid I can't shake this dreadful feeling about the missing key."

Mabel's gold bracelets clinked softly as she reached out to

pat Nan's hand. "Now, now, it's bound to turn up. Have you asked Bumbles? That cheeky little pixie sees everything that goes on around here."

"Brilliant idea!" Nan exclaimed, her spirits momentarily lifted. She rose and leaned out the open window, calling out in a sing-song voice: "Bumbles, darling! Might we have a word?"

In a twinkling the impish pixie appeared, his glamour making him look like an unusually vibrant bumblebee. His large eyes flickered with roguery as he hovered before Nan.

"Bumbles," Nan began, her voice tinged with desperation, "have you or any of your kin seen the house key? I left it on the dining room table last night attached to my long silver chain, and now it's vanished without a trace."

Bumbles furrowed his tiny brow in puzzlement, his wings buzzing louder as he considered. "Hmm, a missing key, you say? Quite the mystery! Rest assured, Lady Nan, the pixie network is on the case. Nothing escapes our notice—or our tiny fingers." He touched his forehead in a somber salute before zipping off in a blur of iridescent light, calling back over his shoulder, "Unless one of the goblins has it, in which case all bets are off!"

Nan sighed, sinking back into her chair. "What if I've lost it for good?" she fretted.

Mabel's voice cut through her gloomy concerns. "While we wait, shall we delve into Bithia's diary? Perhaps it will offer some insight into Cordelia's... predicament."

Nan nodded, reaching for the worn leather-bound book. As she opened it the musty scent of aged paper filled the air, mingling with the delicate aroma of their blinis. She cleared her throat and began to read aloud:

"'I fear something is terribly amiss with my dear sister. Cordelia's behavior grows more erratic by the day. This morning I found her in the attic amidst a sea of shattered mirrors, their jagged edges glinting like accusations in the dim light. She was muttering feverishly, her words barely coherent —something about 'keeping it out'. When I called her name she turned to me with eyes so wild, so haunted, I scarcely recognized her. My heart aches to think that my love for the unseen world has drawn this shadow into our lives. Oh, how I wish that dreadful séance had never taken place.'"

Nan paused, her voice quavering. "Poor Bithia. The guilt must have been unbearable."

Mabel leaned in, her face a mask of concern. "Indeed. The conjuring of the supernatural can be quite dangerous."

Nan nodded, her fingers tracing the faded ink on the yellowed pages. "Yes, the spirit world was quite active in the Victorian era," she mused. "Perhaps we can finally bring peace to both sisters."

With a deep breath she continued reading, her voice barely above a whisper as she recounted Bithia's growing fear and suspicion of Cordelia's possession. The warm sunlight seemed to dim, casting long shadows across the room as the two friends delved deeper into the tragic tale of the sisters and the malevolent force that tore them apart.

Mabel's hands trembled slightly as she reached for a stack of brittle newspaper clippings.

"Oh my," she exclaimed, her eyes widening as she scanned the headlines. "Listen to this, Nan. 'Local Heiress's Descent into Madness: Strange Occurrences Plague Victorian Manor.'"

Nan leaned forward, frowning. "How dreadful. What else does it say?"

Mabel cleared her throat, her melodic voice taking on a somber tone. "It seems Cordelia's behavior became increasingly alarming. There are reports of her screaming at unseen entities, objects moving of their own accord, and... oh dear... even instances of levitation."

Nan's eyes widened with fear as she remembered the evening when her bed had levitated, scaring Mossy so much that he had left to sleep in the RV. "Levitation?" she repeated in shock. "That's definitely not something anyone would want to experience."

A wry smile played at Mabel's lips. "I daresay it would make for rather interesting dinner conversation, though."

Nan chuckled softly, grateful for her friend's ability to find humor even in the darkest of situations. "How fortunate I am to have you by my side in this ghostly adventure," she said. "But in all seriousness," she continued, her voice taking on a more thoughtful tone, "these occurrences align perfectly with Bithia's diary entries. It seems the revenant's influence over Cordelia grew stronger over time."

Mabel nodded, her fingers absently toying with her layered gold necklaces. "And poor Bithia, watching helplessly as her sister succumbed to this malevolent force. All because of a séance gone awry."

"The weight of her guilt must have been crushing," Nan mused, her hand instinctively reaching for the spot where her missing key should have been. "Oh, Bithia," she mused, "if only you could have foreseen the consequences of that fateful night."

As they continued to piece together the timeline of events, the Victorian manor itself seemed to hold its breath—as if listening intently to the unraveling of its own tragic history.

Nan's fingers trembled as she unfurled another yellowed newspaper clipping. The crystal flute in her other hand teetered precariously, threatening to spill its contents onto the velvet-covered chair.

"Oh, Mabel," she gasped, her voice barely above a whisper. "I think... I think we've found it."

Mabel leaned in, her clasped hands resting softly on the antique table. "What is it, dear?"

Nan cleared her throat, willing her voice not to quaver as she read aloud:

"'Tragedy Strikes: Sisters Perish in Fatal Fall.' Mabel, it's... it's dreadful. Listen to this: 'In a shocking turn of events, twin sisters Bithia and Cordelia met their untimely demise last evening when they plummeted from a third-story window of their family estate. Witnesses report a violent struggle preceded the fall, with Miss Cordelia Croker allegedly pushing her sister before leaping to her own death.'"

Mabel's hand flew to her mouth, her bracelets jingling discordantly. "Good heavens! Cordelia pushed Bithia? But they were sisters!"

Nan nodded grimly, her fingers unconsciously tracing the outline of her pearls. "The revenant's influence must have been absolute by then. Poor Cordelia... poor Bithia."

Their eyes met, a silent understanding passing between them. The weight of the revelation settled heavily in the room.

"To think," Nan mused, "that such darkness dwells within these very walls. Even now, as we sit sipping blinis and unraveling this tragic tale like some macabre mystery novel."

"I suppose," Mabel ventured, breaking the tense silence, "that this puts rather a damper on your plans for a cheery bed and breakfast, doesn't it?"

Despite the severity of the situation Nan let out a small, slightly hysterical laugh. "Oh, Mabel." She sighed, reaching out to squeeze her friend's hand. "Whatever are we going to do?"

Mabel's eyes flashed with determination, her cheerful demeanor reasserting itself. "Well, my dear Nan, I believe we must do what any proper Victorian spiritualists would do in such a situation. We shall cross-reference!"

Nan quirked an eyebrow, her lips curving into a bemused smile. "Cross-reference? And here I thought you might suggest we brew a pot of chamomile tea and call it a day."

"Nonsense," Mabel replied, waving a hand dismissively, her bracelets chiming like fairy bells. "We have Bithia's diary entries and these newspaper clippings. If we compare them, we might uncover more truths about that fateful night. The more information we have, the more powerful we are."

"Mabel dear," Nan cooed fondly, "you approach even the most ghastly of mysteries with the enthusiasm of a garden party planner." She acquiesced, reaching for the leather-bound diary. "As you wish, my dear friend. I'll read from Bithia's account, and you can match it to the news reports."

As Nan's fingers danced across the yellowed pages, she cleared her throat and began to read aloud:

"'Cordelia's behavior grows more erratic by the day. This morning, I found her in the attic, speaking to shadows. When I approached, she turned to me with eyes that were not her own...'"

Mabel rustled through the newspaper clippings, her countenance a study in concentration. "Here!" she exclaimed, holding up a fragile piece of newsprint. "Listen to this, Nan: 'Tragedy Strikes Nettles Manor: Sisters Found Dead, Whispers of Haunting Begin.'"

Nan leaned forward, her heart racing. "Go on, Mabel. What else does it say?"

Nan took a sip of her drink as Mabel continued reading, her voice trembling slightly:

"'In the wake of the Crocker sisters' tragic demise, rumors of supernatural occurrences have gripped our fair town. Several renowned psychics have attempted to cleanse the property, each departing in a state of profound distress. Madame Esmeralda Thornwood, a celebrated medium from New Orleans, was found wandering the beach at dawn, muttering incoherently about 'a darkness that devours light'. The esteemed Dr. Thaddeus Blackwood suffered a complete mental collapse after spending a single night within the mansion's walls, babbling about 'eyes in the shadows' before being committed to Bellevue Asylum.'"

"Oh, my," Nan sighed. "It seems our revenant has quite the nasty reputation."

Mabel nodded gravely, her usual cheery demeanor dampened by the weight of their discovery. "Indeed, it does. One wonders how we've managed to coexist with such a malevolent force for so long."

As if in response to Mabel's musings a gentle breeze rustled the velvet drapes, carrying with it the faint scent of jasmine from the garden. Nan found herself drawn to the window, her gaze sweeping across the sun-dappled lawn.

"Perhaps," she mused, more to herself than to Mabel, "we've been protected all this time. By Bithia, or some other benevolent spirit."

Just then, a familiar buzzing sound caught Nan's attention. She turned to see Bumbles, the proud pixie leader, zipping through the open window. His tiny face was scrunched in concentration as he hovered before them.

"Greetings, Lady Nan. Lady Mabel," he squeaked, bowing mid-air. "I regret to inform you that we've not yet located your misplaced key. However, fear not! The pixie brigade stands ready to assist in a most thorough search of the premises."

As if on cue a swarm of glittering, gossamer-winged pixies flooded into the parlor, their tiny forms creating a dazzling display of light and motion. Nan smiled at the sight even as her concern for the missing key gnawed at her.

"Oh, Bumbles," she said, her tone a mixture of gratitude and worry. "You and your kin are too kind. But I do hope we find it soon. I fear what chicanery might occur should it fall into the wrong hands—spectral or otherwise."

Mabel nodded in agreement, her gaze following the pixies as they darted about the room. "Indeed."

As the pixies dispersed throughout the house Bumbles settled onto a nearby doily, his large eyes fixed intently on Nan and Mabel. The ladies exchanged a meaningful glance, silently debating how much to reveal in the presence of their diminutive audience.

Nan took a deep breath, her fingers absently tracing the outline of her crystal glass. The magnitude of their discovery hung gravely in the air.

"Mabel, dear," she began, her voice barely above a whisper, "I fear we've stumbled upon a darkness far more insidious than we initially imagined. Cordelia's revenant is not merely a restless spirit, but a malevolent force that has harassed countless victims."

Mabel leaned back in her chair, shifting her weight. "You're right, Nan. For the sake of Bithia, Cordelia, and all those who've suffered, we must take action."

Bumbles, his tiny ears perked up, piped in with a high-pitched chirp, "Begging your pardon, ladies, but we pixies have some experience with malevolent forces. Perhaps we could be of assistance in your endeavor?"

Nan's eyebrows shot up in surprise. "Why, Bumbles, that's terribly kind of you. But surely this is too dangerous for such delicate creatures?"

The pixie puffed out his chest, looking comically indignant. "I assure you, Lady Nan, we may be small but our magic is potent."

Mabel's eyes gleamed with feverishness. "Nan, don't you see? This could be the answer we've been seeking! A cleansing ritual, led by the pixies! It might just be powerful enough to banish Cordelia's revenant once and for all."

Nan's mind raced with possibilities, a mix of hope and trepidation swirling in her chest. "A cleansing ritual? Oh my, it sounds frightfully exciting. And perhaps a touch dangerous. But if it means freeing poor Cordelia and bringing peace to this house..." She trailed off, her gaze drifting to the newspaper clippings strewn across the table.

"We must try," Mabel said firmly, reaching out to squeeze Nan's hand.

Bumbles fluttered up, his tiny face set with purpose. "Leave the preparations to us, ladies. We'll gather the necessary elements from the garden and align the cosmic energies. All we ask is that you lend your human will and intention to the ritual at noon tomorrow."

Nan nodded, feeling a surge of courage. "Very well, then. Let us prepare to face this revenant and reclaim our home from the shadows of the past."

As Bumbles zipped off to rally more of his kin, Nan wondered what otherworldly challenges awaited them. But with Mabel by her side and an army of pixies at their back, she felt ready to confront whatever spectral horrors lurked within the walls.

Mabel's sun hat bobbed as she rose from her seat, her eyes sparkling. "I'll dash home and gather the flowers we need, dear. Rosemary for remembrance, angelica for inspiration, mint for protection, eucalyptus to banish negative energies..." She counted off on her fingers, her voice trailing into a melodious hum. "Bumbles will need some flower reinforcements."

Nan nodded, tucking her hair behind her ear. "Who would have thought your penchant for Victorian flower language would come in handy for ghost-banishing?"

As Mabel bustled towards the door, her wicker basket swinging on her arm, Nan called after her, "See you tomorrow, darling. I'll set up candles throughout the house. It'll be like a séance straight out of Bithia's diary!"

With Mabel gone Nan set about her task, her heeled sandals clicking against the polished wooden floors. As she placed delicate tapers in antique holders, she mused aloud, "Oh, Bithia, just hold on. We are preparing to banish the revenant!"

A chill breeze rustled the lace curtains, and Nan fancied she heard a whisper of approval. She continued, her voice carrying a hint of whimsy, "We simply must banish this revenant before we open the B&B. Can you imagine the reviews? 'Lovely breakfast, shame about the malevolent spirit trying to possess us over tea.'"

Nan chuckled at her own jest, but her eyes held a serious glint. "Once we've cleared the air so to speak, perhaps you and Cordelia can find peace here, Bithia. And who knows? Maybe you'll even become our spectral concierges. Mr. Nettles would certainly prefer friendly ghosts to vengeful ones."

As she placed the final candle, Nan's thoughts turned to her husband. "Oh, Mossy," she murmured, sighing, "if only you could appreciate the magic that surrounds us. But don't worry, darling. We'll make this home safe for all—the living, the dead, and even the reluctant."

As if in response to Nan's musings a shimmering cloud of light spilled through the open window, dappling the parlor walls in a kaleidoscope of gold and silver. The air hummed with the faint music of fluttering wings as hundreds of pixies swirled in, their forms shimmering like morning dew in the sun. At their center, cradled reverently by a dozen of the smallest fae, dangled the tarnished key on its silver chain, catching the light like a fragment of moonlight brought to earth.

Nan's eyes widened, her heart quickening. "Oh, you clever little darlings!" she exclaimed, her voice filled with delight and relief. "You've found it!"

The pixies deposited the key gently into her outstretched palm. Its weight felt familiar, almost alive in her hand. Nan examined it closely, admiring again the intricate Victorian filigree work along its shaft.

Bumbles stepped forward, his voice ringing clear, "It was hiding in the attic."

"Well, I never," she breathed, her thoughts racing. "Hidden

away in the attic. Bithia, you sly fox. Did you put it there for safekeeping?"

With reverent care Nan slipped the long silver chain over her head, the key settling against her chest. A warmth spread through her body, as if the house itself was sighing in contentment.

Turning to face the room at large, pixies still swirling about her like stardust, Nan raised her voice in a solemn vow. "To this house and all who dwell within, both seen and unseen," she began, her voice steady but filled with emotion, "I make this solemn vow. This key shall remain with me, not as a trinket or curiosity but as a promise—a reminder of the magic that binds us, the history that breathes through these walls, and the love that makes this house a home. Together we shall protect this sanctuary and all who seek solace within it, in this life and beyond."

Pizza and Wine

The soft glow of candlelight danced across the formal dining room, casting flickering shadows that seemed to waltz in time with Nat King Cole's velvet voice emanating from the record player. Nan sat at the table, her white knit set a bright focal point against the deep mahogany that dominated the room, the house key a talisman against her chest. Across from her, Mossy's eyes blazed like sapphires in the low light, his dark blue sweater making them impossibly bluer.

"Darling, you simply can't pour me another glass," Nan protested, a giggle threatening to escape her lips. "I've already indulged far too much this evening."

Mossy arched an eyebrow mischievously as he reached for the bottle of rosé. "My dear Nan, when it comes to pizza night there's no such thing as too much indulgence. Besides, this wine has a history as rich as its flavor."

Nan leaned forward, captivated by the way Mossy's eyes lit up when he spoke of his passions. She thought, not for the first time, how his voice could make even the driest of subjects sound like poetry.

"You see," Mossy continued, "around Lake Garda, where Veneto and Lombardy meet, rosato has been a tradition for over a century. They call it Chiaretto there—'light' or 'pale'. It's been made since 1896, making it one of Italy's oldest rosé regions."

"Oh, Mossy." Nan sighed, her heart swelling with affection. "I do so love our pizza nights. Such a delightful indulgence. I could listen to you talk about Italy all evening."

Mossy's lips quirked into a fond smile. "And I, my dear, could listen to your charming compliments all night. It seems a touch of wine brings out the minx in you."

Nan felt a blush creeping up her cheeks, remembering the spirits that truly did roam their halls. "Well then," she said, pushing her glass towards him with a coy smile. "Pour away, love. But do be warned—a sassy Nan might just sweep you off your feet."

As Mossy filled her glass, his fingers brushed hers. In that touch Nan felt the magnitude of their shared history, the promise of adventures yet to come, and the comforting knowledge that, ghostly houseguests notwithstanding, she was precisely where she belonged.

As the rich, velvety tones of Nat King Cole's "Unforgettable" filled the air, Mossy's eyes lit up with a mischievous gleam. He rose from his chair, his silver-white hair falling charmingly over his brow, and extended his hand to Nan.

"My darling," he crooned, matching the melody, "shall we dance?"

Nan's heart fluttered as she placed her hand in his. "Why, Mr. Nettles, I thought you'd never ask."

With surprising grace Mossy swept Nan into his arms, twirling her away from the table. Their laughter mingled with the music as they glided across the weathered wooden floor, its soft creaks a percussion to their impromptu waltz.

"Oh!" Nan gasped as Mossy dipped her low, the key

around her neck swinging free. For a moment, she swore she saw Bithia's approving smile in the flickering candlelight.

As they swayed Nan nestled closer to Mossy, inhaling the scent of old books and sea salt that clung to his sweater. "You're full of surprises tonight, my love," she murmured.

Mossy's eyes twinkled behind his spectacles. "A man must keep some mysteries, even from his observant wife."

Their dance ended with a flourish, both slightly breathless and giddy. They returned to the table, where the remaining slices of Stavro's pizza sat on Nan's prized Wedgwood china.

"My word," Nan chuckled, lifting a slice onto her plate. "Grandmother would have a conniption if she saw pizza lounging on her Wedgwood. She always insisted these plates were 'for heirs and dignitaries only'."

Mossy grinned, swirling his wine. "And here we are, commoners with impeccable taste, proving her wrong."

As Nan savored a bite of the pizza, she pondered the dichotomy before her—the charm of antique china juxtaposed with the casual, modern comfort food. It was, she realized, a perfect representation of their life together: Mossy's laid-back scholarly nature complementing her love for the unknown, creating a harmony as sweet as any ghostly melody.

Nan dabbed her lips with a linen napkin. "Darling, tell me about your day. I've been dying to know how the renovations are progressing."

Mossy leaned back in his chair, a contented sigh escaping his lips. "Ah, my dear, it was a day of triumphs and tribulations. The attic window, that stubborn old thing, finally yielded to my persistence. It now opens with nary a creak, ready to welcome the sea breeze."

"Oh, how delightful!" Nan exclaimed, applauding her husband. "And what of the guest bedroom? I've been ever so eager to see it finished."

"You'll be pleased to know, my love, that it's coming

along splendidly," Mossy replied, his voice taking on a dreamy quality. "The new chandelier—a delightful confection of crystal and brass—now hangs like a constellation of stars against the freshly painted ceiling. And the floor is no longer a shabby affair, but gleams with the warmth of honey."

Nan leaned forward, entranced. "And the wallpaper?"

"Ah, the wallpaper!" Mossy's eyes lit up. "A pattern of climbing roses and hidden faeries, just as you wished. The walls themselves have come alive with whimsy."

As Mossy spoke, Nan found herself transported to the room in her mind's eye. She could almost smell the fresh paint and feel the smooth, refinished floors beneath her feet. But there was more to share, and her heart quickened with excitement.

"Mossy, dear," she began, her voice trembling slightly, "while you've been breathing new life into our home, Mabel and I have been unearthing its past."

Mossy raised an eyebrow, intrigued. "Do tell, my curious cat. What secrets have you coaxed from these old walls?"

Nan took a deep breath, her fingers unconsciously playing with the key around her neck. "We've discovered the truth about Bithia. Oh, Mossy, it's terribly tragic! She was a celebrated spiritualist, you see, but her gift was her downfall."

As Nan recounted Bithia's story, her eyes shone with a mix of sadness and wonder. "But that's not all," she continued, leaning in conspiratorially. "We've devised a plan to banish the Relevant—with the help of pixies!"

Mossy's eyebrows shot up, disappearing beneath his snowy fringe. "Pixies, you say?" He leaned back with a wry grin, swirling the last of his wine. "Should I start leaving out saucers of cream for our new landlords? Or would whiskey suit them better?"

Nan laughed, the tinkling sound filling the room. "Oh,

you! Just you wait and see. Tomorrow we'll set things right in this house, and Bithia will finally be at peace."

As she spoke, Nan marveled at the strange turns her life had taken. Here she was, planning supernatural interventions over pizza and fine wine, with the most wonderfully understanding husband by her side. It was, she thought, exactly the sort of delightful madness she had always dreamed of.

Mossy's eyes softened as he reached across the table to take Nan's hand. With a twinkle of roguery he lifted it to his lips, his breath warm against her skin. "My brave darling," he murmured, "your fanciful spirit never ceases to amaze me."

With deliberate slowness he pushed up her sleeve, laying a trail of feather-light kisses along her arm. Nan's breath caught in her throat, her skin tingling at his touch. Gratitude filled her heart. After all these years, Mossy could still make her heart flutter like a lovestruck teenager.

"Pixies or no pixies," he continued, his voice a low, velvety rumble, "if it brings you joy, then I am content." He cradled her face in his hands. "For, as the Bard himself said, 'Love looks not with the eyes, but with the mind, and therefore is winged Cupid painted blind.'"

Nan felt herself melting into his gaze, thinking how perfectly Mossy embodied both the scholar and the romantic. "Oh, you silver-tongued devil," she whispered, her cheeks flushing with warmth that had nothing to do with the wine.

Mossy chuckled, rising to his feet with a slight wobble that betrayed the influence of the Chiaretto. "Now then, my pixie-whispering enchantress," he said, a playful lilt in his voice, "how might I assist in this supernatural scheme of yours?"

As he spoke, Nan could see the gears turning in his wine-addled mind. She braced herself, knowing what was coming.

"Did you know," Mossy began, his eyes taking on that familiar, faraway look, "that the belief in fairy folk dates back to ancient times? The Celts, for instance, believed in creatures called sidhe..."

Nan settled back in her chair, a fond smile on her face as she listened to her husband's impromptu lecture. She thought to herself, *This is precisely why I fell in love with him—his brilliant mind, his unwavering support and, yes, even his tipsy tangents on folklore.*

Nan traced the edge of her wine glass as she listened to Mossy's enthusiastic ramblings about fairy lore. The candlelight cast dancing shadows across his animated features, and she found herself momentarily mesmerized by the interplay of light and shadow. With a gentle sigh, she knew it was time to broach the subject at hand.

"Darling," Nan interjected softly. "As fascinating as the sidhe are, I'm afraid I must ask for your trust in something rather... unusual."

Mossy set down his glass, tilting his head with amused curiosity. "You have my trust, Nan, but now you have my attention. What's on your mind, my dear?"

Nan took a deep breath, the key around her neck feeling heavier. "I need you to be out of the house tomorrow at noon. It's... well, it's for the banishing ritual."

Confusion clouded Mossy's features.

"It's to do with Bithia and the Relevant," Nan explained, her voice taking on a hint of urgency. "We must perform the ritual without any... interference."

Mossy's lips quirked into a bemused smile. "Interference? Surely you don't mean me, dearest?"

"I'm afraid I do," Nan insisted, reaching across the table to clasp his hand. "Please, Mossy. It's important."

A moment of silence stretched between them, broken only by the soft crackle of the candle flames. Then Mossy's expression softened, and he kissed the back of Nan's hand.

"Very well, my enigmatic beauty," he murmured against

her skin. "Far be it from me to stand in the way of your super-natural endeavors. But tell me," he added, his eyes glinting mischievously, "is there perhaps something I can do tonight to ease your worries?"

Nan felt a delightful shiver run up her arm as Mossy traced lazy circles on her palm with his thumb. "Mr. Nettles," she breathed, "are you attempting to seduce me?"

"Attempting?" Mossy chuckled, rising from his chair with surprising grace for a man who'd imbibed so much wine. He pulled Nan to her feet, drawing her close. "My darling, I should hope I'm succeeding."

Nan's heart fluttered as she gazed up at Mossy, his eyes filled with mirth and desire. She felt herself melting into his embrace, the warmth of the wine and the intoxicating scent of his cologne making her head spin delightfully.

"Oh, you impossible man," she whispered, her fingers tracing the soft wool of his sweater. "You know I can't resist when you quote poetry at me."

Mossy's chest rumbled with a low laugh. "Then allow me to render you utterly helpless, my love." He leaned in close, his breath tickling her ear as he recited, "'My bounty is as boundless as the sea, My love as deep. The more I give to thee, The more I have, for both are infinite.'"

Nan felt her knees go weak. "Shakespeare," she breathed. "You do know how to make a girl swoon."

"I should hope so," Mossy replied, his hand sliding to the small of her back. "After all, what good is a gentleman's education if not to woo his lady fair?"

As they swayed gently to the fading notes of Nat King Cole, Nan appreciated Mossy's gentle arms. They grounded her in a world filled with ghosts and pixies. She sighed, pressing her cheek to his chest.

Mossy's voice broke through her reverie. "Shall we retire to more... comfortable quarters, my dear? I believe I have a few more verses that might interest you."

Nan felt a delicious thrill of desire. "Lead on, Mr. Nettles. I'm all yours."

With a playful flourish, Mossy took her hand and guided her up the stairs and toward the bedroom. As they reached the doorway he paused, a mischievous glint in his eye.

"Remember, my love," he quoted, his voice rich with amusement and affection, "The course of true love never did run smooth. But I daresay, we're doing a fine job of navigating its twists and turns."

Nan's laughter echoed as Mossy swept her into the bedroom, the door closing softly behind them.

The gentle glow of the bedside lamp cast a warm, intimate light across the room, softening the edges of their silhouettes.

Mossy's long, elegant fingers found their way to the key dangling from the silver chain around Nan's neck. "My dearest Nan," he murmured, his voice low and rich like aged whiskey, "as the Bard himself said, 'Love looks not with the eyes, but with the mind.'"

"And what does your mind see, my love?" Nan asked, her breath catching as Mossy moved to cup her cheek.

"A world of wonder," he replied, pulling her close. "And at its center, you."

Staircases and Specters

A crash shattered the velvety stillness, the sound of breaking china ricocheting through the house. Nan jolted upright, her heart pounding as the room seemed to tremble in the moonlight, its silvery glow twisting the floral patterns of the Victorian wallpaper into something sinister.

Her heart raced as she fumbled for the bedside lamp, her fingers trembling.

"Mossy!" she cried, her voice quavering. "Mossy, wake up!"

Mossy stirred, his hair tousled. "What's happening, my dear? Is it the spirits again?"

Another violent shake rattled the windows. Nan clutched the folds of her chintz nightgown, the smooth cotton a fragile comfort against the goosebumps creeping up her arms. *We cannot let the house win*, she thought, though her bare feet hesitated against the cool wooden floor. "We must investigate," she declared, forcing a steadiness into her voice she didn't quite feel.

Mossy, now alert, swung his striped-pajama-clad legs out of bed. "Right you are, my love. Lead on, intrepid ghosthunter."

As they ventured into the hallway, bathed in an other-worldly blue glow, Nan's mind raced. What new spectral mischief was afoot in their beloved abode? She reached for Mossy's hand, drawing strength from his presence.

A sudden pressure, cold and invisible, pressed against Nan's back. It wasn't a shove—more like a creeping malice that sent her reeling forward. She cried out, her arms flailing in a futile attempt to catch the banister before the staircase rose to meet her in a series of brutal thuds.

Time seemed to slow as Nan tumbled down the stairs, each thud of her body against the polished wood a dull echo in her ears. Mossy's horrified gasp barely registered as she came to rest at the middle of the long staircase, a tangle of limbs and cotton nightgown.

"Nanette!" Mossy's voice was thick with concern as he hurried down the steps. "Are you all right, my darling?"

Dazed, Nan blinked up at him, her curls askew. "I... I believe I've been pushed by our ghostly tenant," she managed, attempting a weak smile. "How dreadfully rude."

As Mossy helped her sit up, Nan couldn't shake the feeling that this was more than the revenant's usual pranks. Something had changed in their ghostly haven, and she was bent on uncovering the truth. After a cup of tea and an ice pack, of course.

Mossy's eyes flashed with indignation, his hair standing on end. He gently helped Nan to her feet then whirled to face the empty air, his fist raised dramatically towards the ceiling.

"Now see here, you specter of ill manners!" he bellowed, stepping forward with all the indignation of a stage actor addressing an unruly audience. "Is this your grand performance? Disturbing slumber and toppling a lady from her perch? This shall not stand! As Prospero commanded the tempest, so I command you: begone, foul miscreant!"

Mossy gestured wildly as he continued his impromptu

soliloquy. "As the Bard himself once penned, 'We are such stuff as dreams are made on.' But how, pray tell, are we to dream when you insist on this nocturnal nonsense?"

A chill wind whipped through the hallway, causing the lace curtains to dance an eerie waltz.

Mossy pressed on undeterred, his voice rising to a crescendo. "I demand you cease this tomfoolery at once! Or, as Hamlet so eloquently put it, 'Rest, rest, perturbed spirit!'"

As the last echoes of Mossy's impassioned speech faded, an unnatural stillness fell over the house. The air seemed to thicken, and Nan could have sworn she saw a shimmering outline materialize before them.

"Mossy," she whispered, tugging at his pajama sleeve, "I believe our uninvited guest may be... listening."

The shimmering outline dissipated, leaving behind a chill in the air.

Still reeling from her tumble down the stairs Nan clung to the banister, her knuckles paling against the cool, polished wood. The faint scent of beeswax rose from the railing, grounding her as the room spun around her. Each step was a precarious negotiation, her trembling legs testing the strength of her footing against the creaking, treacherous stairs.

"Oh, bother," she muttered under her breath, her usual theatrical flair subdued by the throbbing in her ankle. "I feel rather like Alice tumbling down the rabbit hole, only with considerably less whimsy and far more bruising."

Mossy, his righteous indignation giving way to concern, turned from his ghostly audience to his wife.

He peered through narrowed eyes, unable to see clearly without his glasses as he took in Nan's unsteady progress.

"My dear!" he exclaimed, leaning her into his side with ample agility. "Are you quite all right? Let me assist you, my darling Dulcinea."

Nan smiled at his reference despite her discomfort. "Dulcinea, is it? Well then, my gallant Don Quixote, I'd be most grateful for your chivalrous aid."

With gentle care Mossy wrapped an arm around Nan's waist, supporting her as they made their way down the remaining steps. The weathered floorboards creaked beneath their feet, a familiar melody in the quieting house.

"I do hope," Nan whispered conspiratorially as they shuffled towards the kitchen, "that our spectral friend appreciated your dramatic flair. It was quite the performance, my love."

Mossy chuckled softly, guiding her to a chair in the cozy kitchen. "Well, one must rise to the occasion when addressing the spirit world. Though I confess I'm beginning to wonder if we might need to schedule our hauntings. Perhaps set up a ghostly appointment book?"

As Nan eased into the chair, wincing slightly, she pondered the absurdity of their situation.

"Oh, Mossy," she sighed, a mix of amusement and exasperation in her voice, "whatever shall we do with our uninvited guests? I'm starting to think we may need to brush up on our séance etiquette."

With a flick of his fingers upon the light switch Mossy illuminated the kitchen, bathing the room in a warm, buttery glow. The light danced off the polished surfaces, casting playful shadows that seemed to waltz with the lingering wisps of spectral energy.

"Now, my dear," Mossy said, his voice as soft as the moonlight that had guided them moments before, "let's tend to that ankle of yours. We can't have our leading lady limping about, can we?"

He filled the basin with water, his fingers trembling ever so slightly as he worked. Nan, perched on the edge of the chair, watched him with fond amusement despite the throbbing in her ankle. "Perhaps I should embrace the role of the tragic heroine," she quipped, her eyes sparkling. "A mysterious limp would lend our B&B a certain gothic flair, don't you think?"

Mossy's laughter rumbled through the kitchen as he knelt before her, reminiscent of a knight before his lady. "My darling, you're quite intriguing enough without resorting to theatrical injuries."

As he carefully wrapped the cool, damp cloth around her ankle, Nan relished the tenderness of his touch. His long fingers worked with a dexterity that belied their size, and she found herself wondering not for the first time at the contradiction that was her beloved Mossy.

"I do hope," Nan said, wincing slightly as he adjusted the cloth, "that our spectral housemates appreciate the disruption they've caused to our beauty sleep. Though I suppose, being incorporeal, they have little need for such mortal concerns."

Mossy looked up at her. "Perhaps we should leave out a ghostly cup of tea next time. One wonders," he mused, his fingers drumming theatrically on the counter, "whether our incorporeal guests would prefer the boldness of an Earl Grey or the civility of an English Breakfast. Perhaps a dash of sugar to sweeten their disposition?"

His expression shifted, the mirth in his eyes replaced by a smoldering intensity. He rose to his feet as he gazed down at Nan. "My dearest," he began, his voice low and resonant, "while our uninvited guests may lack corporeal form, they shall not lack for a stern talking-to."

Nan watched as her husband's chest swelled with indignation, his hands curling into fists at his sides. "These spectral miscreants may have the advantage of passing through walls, but they shall not pass through the fortress of our resolve," Mossy declared, his words lush with fervor.

A small smile tugged at Nan's lips despite the throbbing in her ankle. "Oh, Mossy," she sighed, her voice tinged with both amusement and admiration. "You do have a way with words, my love."

Mossy's gaze softened as he looked at her, "We shall prevail, Nan," he said, kneeling once more and taking her hands in his. "This home, our sanctuary, will not be surrendered to ethereal interlopers. No matter how persistent they may be."

Nan squeezed Mossy's hands, marveling at how his touch could make her feel so safe even in the face of supernatural chaos. "Together, then?" she asked, her eyes searching his.

"Always, my dear," he replied, his voice as warm and comforting as a crackling fire. "We shall face these phantasmal foes with all the courage and wit at our disposal. And perhaps," he added with a wry smile, "a dash of that famous Nettles charm."

Mossy placed his hands upon his hips. "Now," he declared, "I believe this situation calls for a restorative cup of tea. Allow me to demonstrate my culinary prowess, or lack thereof."

With a flourish that would have befitted a Victorian conjurer, Mossy set about preparing the tea tray. Nan watched him with fond amusement as he fumbled with the cups and saucers, his fingers clumsy in their domestic endeavor.

"My darling," Mossy said, narrowly avoiding disaster as he caught a falling teaspoon, "I fear I must confess that my talents lie more in the realm of the written word than in the kitchen. How fortunate I am to have such a bewitching beauty of a wife with such feminine wiles to compensate for my short-comings."

Nan laughed, wincing slightly as the movement jostled her injured ankle. "Oh, Mossy," she replied, her voice rich with affection, "you know what they say: 'The way to a man's heart is through his stomach'."

"Ah, but we men are simple creatures with basic needs," Mossy quipped, setting the kettle on the stove with exaggerated care. "A warm hearth, a good book, and the company of an enchanting wife—what more could one ask for?"

As Mossy busied himself with the tea preparations, Nan found herself reflecting on the curious path that had led them to this moment. How strange, she thought, that a Victorian spiritualist's legacy should bring such excitement—and pain—into their lives. Yet as she watched her husband's endearingly awkward attempts at domesticity, she couldn't imagine facing these supernatural trials with anyone else by her side.

"Mossy," she called softly, "do be a dear and fetch an ice pack for my ankle while the tea steeps. I fear our spectral assailant has left me somewhat the worse for wear."

"At once, my love," Mossy replied, his voice filled with gentle concern. He retrieved the ice pack from the freezer, handling it as carefully as if it were a rare manuscript. Kneeling once more before Nan, he gently placed the cold compress on her swollen ankle.

"Whatever would I do without you, Mossy Nettles?" Nan murmured, her words hanging in the air like a tender incantation.

With gratitude, she received her tea from Mossy and brought it to her lips. The chamomile's warmth enveloped her like a soothing hug. Her eyes, still bright despite the evening's trials, locked onto Mossy's sheepish gaze. "My dear," she said, her voice carrying the theatrical lilt that so often colored her speech, "your ministrations are nothing short of miraculous."

Mossy's cheeks flushed with a hint of pink, visible even in the buttery glow of the kitchen light. He straightened his posture, a familiar glimmer of passion igniting in his eyes. "Ah, my sweet Nan," he began, his words emerging with the careful precision of a poet, "we are but players on this spectral stage, facing challenges that would make lesser souls quake with fear."

He began to pace, his movements taking on the exaggerated swagger of Cervantes' famous knight-errant. "We shall tilt at these windmills of the supernatural, my dear Dulcinea," he declared, brandishing an imaginary lance, "and emerge victorious, restoring tranquility to our beloved home!"

As Mossy's impassioned performance echoed through the kitchen, Nan's heart swelled with love and exasperation. Even amid ghostly mischief, his unwavering spirit remained her constant—eccentric, poetic, and wonderfully hers. She reached for his hand, her fingers curling around his like ivy. "Oh, Mossy," she murmured, her voice soft. "What a marvelous oddity you are."

The Revenant Revealed

The late-morning Florida sun painted the sky in hues of lavender and gold, its soft light catching on the pristine white paint of the Nettles' Victorian home. The porch boards creaked beneath Nan's sandals, their gentle protests blending with the distant trill of a mockingbird.

Nan's fingers traced the ornate key hanging from her neck, a constant reminder of the spectral world that danced just beyond mortal sight. She turned to Mossy, her husband's sky-blue shirt a complement to the warm tones of morning.

"My dearest rose, guard well our abode," Mossy intoned, his voice rich with poetic cadence. "For spirits stir and mysteries unfold, while you chase shadows in the day grown old."

Nan smiled, a mix of fondness and exasperation coloring her features. "Mossy, darling, your verse is as charming as ever," she teased, brushing a curl from her face. "But don't let your poetic musings distract you from the task at hand. The freshest eggs, if you please."

Mossy, adjusting his gold aviator sunglasses with a flourish, grinned. "Fear not, my muse. I shall return with eggs so fresh the hens might file a missing persons report."

As Nan handed him the grocery list, her thoughts wandered to the mission ahead. "A revenant banishment before teatime. How frightfully Victorian of us," she mused. "Do enjoy your day about," she murmured, planting a kiss on Mossy's cheek.

Mossy's penny loafers squeaked softly as he descended the porch steps. "I have faith in you, my dear. You'll sort out this spiritual kerfuffle with all the grace of a duchess at a ball."

Nan watched him go, the canister of salt bulky in her hands. "If only the Victorians could see us now." She smiled. "What would they make of their once-illustrious séance parlor turned supernatural battleground?"

Her reverie was broken by the tinkling of Mabel's jewelry, accompanied by the delicate flutter of pixie wings. Nan turned to see her friend approaching the garden fountain, resplendent in a purple sundress that seemed to dance with every step.

"Nan, darling!" Mabel called, her excitement palpable. "Are we ready to give this revenant the old heave-ho?"

Bumbles, his tiny form glowing like a fragment of captured sunlight, darted from the folds of Mabel's jangling bracelets. "We've summoned every pixie this side of the Atlantic!" he declared, his voice as bright and sharp as a crystal bell. "No spirit stands a chance against our shenanigans!"

Nan smiled at their enthusiasm. "Well then, shall we convene our little ghostbusting tea party? I dare say the revenant has overstayed its welcome."

As they gathered by the fountain, its gentle melody masking their words from prying spectral ears, Nan felt a twinge of destiny. She took a deep breath, the key around her neck seeming to pulse with an otherworldly energy. "Right then, my dears," she began, her voice low and calm. "Our plan is as follows: we shall trap this nefarious revenant in Mabel's coffee tin and give it a proper burial beneath the roses."

Mabel nodded vigorously, her oversized pearl earrings bobbing precariously. "Oh, how poetic! Grounding that nasty energy in Mother Earth herself. Much better than letting it float about, menacing some other poor soul's abode."

"Precisely," Nan agreed. "Now, my little pixie friends, I have a terribly important task for you." She held out the canister of salt, its contents glinting in the sunlight. "We need a circle of salt around the entire property. Think you're up for the challenge?"

Bumbles puffed out his tiny chest. "Yes indeed, my lady!"

As the pixies set to work Nan turned to Mabel. "I've already placed hoplite, tourmaline, and agate at the cardinal points," Nan explained, lowering her voice as if revealing a state secret. "A little guidance from the internet, if you can believe it. Victorian séances meet 21st-century search engines —a truly eclectic collaboration."

Mabel's eyes widened. "The internet? My word, Nan, you are becoming quite the modern woman!"

Nan felt a blush creep up her cheeks. "Well, one must adapt with the times, mustn't one? Even in matters of the supernatural."

Just then a group of pixies returned, their arms laden with delicate crowns woven from lavender and sage. With great ceremony, they placed the fragrant circlets upon Nan and Mabel's heads.

"For protection," one pixie chirped, "and a dash of style!"

Nan touched the crown gently, feeling its soothing energy. "Oh, Mabel," she murmured as she looked to the house, "I do hope Bithia will approve of our methods."

"We will be as gentle as we can be," Mabel assured.

"Now then," Nan said aloud, squaring her shoulders, "shall we face our spectral squatter?"

Mabel linked her arm through Nan's, her countenance filled with bravery and fortitude. "Lead on, my dear. Let's show this revenant that the ladies of Daytona are not to be trifled with!"

As they made their way towards the house, a grin crossed Nan's face. "Ghost hunting in floral crowns and pearls. Agatha Christie would have a field day with us."

Mabel let out a barking laugh.

As Nan and Mabel crossed the threshold into the parlor, they were greeted by a sea of flickering candlelight. White tapers stood sentinel in ornate candelabras, while delicate tealights winked from every available surface. The sea breeze, scented with jasmine and salt, wafted through the open windows, causing the flames to dance and cast enchanting shadows across the room.

"Oh, Nan," Mabel breathed, her eyes wide with wonder. "It's like stepping into a still-life painting!"

Nan smiled, her heart swelling with pride. "I daresay our little gathering might be a tad more lively than usual."

Mabel settled into a plush armchair, her sundress billowing around her. "Speaking of affairs, did I tell you about the time my grandmother attended one of Bithia's famous séances? Right here in this very room!"

As Mabel launched into her tale a familiar chill brushed the back of Nan's neck, raising the fine hairs along her arms. She turned, her breath catching as Bithia's spectral form shimmered into view near the fireplace. The soft glow of her presence seemed to brighten the room, her translucent figure framed by the flickering candlelight like an apparition from a dream. But something was different this time—Mabel froze, her eyes growing impossibly wide.

"Nan," Mabel whispered, her voice trembling, "I... I can see her!"

Bithia's ghostly face broke into a radiant smile. "My, my,"

she said, her voice like wind chimes in a gentle breeze. "You're the spitting image of your grandmother, my dear. How wonderful to see you both."

Nan felt tears prick at her eyes. "Bithia, you remember Mabel's grandmother?"

"Of course." Bithia chuckled. "How could I forget? Those were truly wonderful days."

The air thickened abruptly, carrying a cold that stabbed like needles against Nan's skin. A furious wind seemed to rise from nowhere, tossing candle flames into a wild dance. The delicate china on the mantel shivered violently, their soft clinks turning into a discordant chorus that filled the room.

Bithia's expression darkened. "It's here," she whispered.

Nan reached out, her fingers passing through Bithia's spectral form. "Don't worry," she said, her voice steady despite the fear coiling in her stomach. "We'll free Cordelia from this monstrous revenant. I promise you."

No sooner had the words left her lips than chaos erupted. The parlor door burst open with a resounding crack, revealing the twisted, wraith-like form of Cordelia. Her eyes blazed with otherworldly malevolence.

"Mabel, duck!" Nan cried as a heavy tome went sailing across the room. She dropped to the floor, her heart pounding as she watched chairs and tables begin to levitate, spinning in a dizzying whirlwind around the possessed Cordelia.

Mabel scrambled behind an overturned chaise longue, her pupils dilated with terror. "I always wanted to see a spirit," she shouted over the cacophony, "but this is quite a lot!"

Nan let out a chuckle despite the seriousness of the situation. "Be careful what you wish for, my dear!" she called back, dodging a particularly vicious attack from a rogue candlestick.

The storm of chaos was pierced by a high, musical giggle, sharp as sunlight breaking through storm clouds. Bumbles darted into the fray, his gossamer wings trailing iridescent light. Around him, pixies swirled in a flurry of color, weaving patterns of glowing energy that tangled in the path of the flying objects, turning their menace into a chaotic dance. "Time for some pixie mischief!" he squeaked, his voice barely audible above the commotion.

With a flick of his tiny hand, Bumbles summoned a swarm of pixies that resembled glowing fireflies. They buzzed around Cordelia's head, their lights pulsing in a dizzying pattern. The possessed spirit swatted at them, momentarily distracted from her assault on the room.

"Mabel!" Nan called out, her voice tinged with excitement. "Do you remember that passage from Madame Blavatsky's *Isis Unveiled*? About the power of collective energy?"

Mabel's face lit up with understanding. "Oh, yes! 'The united breath of a pure circle, when directed by a strong will, creates a whirlwind in the astral atmosphere,'" she recited, her words laced with the whimsy of fairy tales and the gravity of Victorian occultism.

As they spoke the pixies joined Bumbles in his efforts, creating tiny illusions of spectral butterflies and ghostly roses that danced around Cordelia, further confusing and aggravating the revenant.

Nan felt the key around her neck grow warm. She grasped it tightly, her mind racing. "Mabel, quick! Join hands with me. We need to create a circle of pure intention around Cordelia!"

Nan took a deep breath, her eyes fixed on Cordelia's writhing form. The room crackled with eerie energy but Nan's voice remained steady, infused with a gentle strength. "Cordelia," she called softly, "I know you're in there, beneath the revenant's hold. Can you hear me? My name is Nan, and this is my friend Mabel. We are friends of your sister Bithia. We're here to help you."

The spirit's hollow, flickering eyes hesitated, a sliver of recognition at the sound of her sister's name softening her malevolent glare. Her spectral form trembled, the jagged edges of her shadowed figure wavering like a mirage.

Nan tightened her grip on Mabel's hand, grounding herself in the warmth of their connection. "Your sister Bithia," she continued, her tone laced with gentle urgency, "loved you dearly. She still does. This anger, this jealousy—it's not you, Cordelia. It's the revenant feeding on your pain, twisting it against you."

Cordelia's shrouded form shuddered violently, her tattered lace gown rippling as though caught in a storm's gale. Her voice emerged as a jagged hiss, an anguished blend of fury and sorrow. "You know nothing of my suffering!" she spat, her words slicing through the emotionally-charged air.

Nan's heart ached, her empathy blossoming like a warm flame against the icy tendrils of despair. "Oh, but I do," she replied, her voice soft and unwavering like the steady warmth of a cup of Earl Grey on a winter's morning. "To feel unseen, unloved—it's a terrible burden to bear. But you don't have to bear it alone anymore."

As if summoned by the strength of Nan's words, Bithia's ethereal form began to materialize beside them. The soft glow of her presence seemed to soothe the roiling tension in the room. She drifted forward, her eyes shimmering with sorrow and love.

"Cordelia," Bithia said, her voice as tender as a lullaby. "My dear sister, I've always loved you. Your gifts—they were different from mine, yes, but no less extraordinary. I admired you."

Cordelia's spectral figure wavered, the sharp bitterness in her eyes fading into confusion. "But..." her voice cracked, faltering. "But I pushed you, Bithia. Out the window. I... I killed you." Her form flickered as if fractured, her guilt splitting her apart.

Mabel let out a soft gasp. She squeezed Nan's hand tightly, as if anchoring them both in the midst of this fervent storm.

Nan stepped forward, her key glowing faintly as it rested against her chest. Her voice brimmed with understanding. "It wasn't entirely you, Cordelia. The revenant latched on to your pain, your fear, your anger. It fed on those feelings until it drowned out the love you had. But you are stronger than it. You can break free."

Cordelia's face contorted, her features twisting under the weight of her anguish. "After I pushed Bithia," she choked out, her voice breaking with despair, "I... I couldn't bear it, so I jumped. I didn't realize..." A wail tore from her, a haunting sound that echoed through the parlor like a storm breaking against the walls.

The air vibrated with spectral energy, the room trembling as if the house itself shared Cordelia's torment. Around them Bumbles and the pixies moved as one, their collective light forming a shimmering circle around the spirit.

Mabel's voice, tremulous but resolute, broke the stillness. "Cordelia, listen to them," she implored, her free hand clutching the lavender crown atop her head. "We're all here to help. You're not alone anymore."

The pixies, their delicate forms glowing like embers, buzzed in unison, their collective magic creating a gentle hum that resonated through the parlor. Cordelia's spectral form began to soften, the jagged edges smoothing as light replaced the dark. Her eyes, once hollow and vengeful, filled with tears.

Bithia moved closer, her arms outstretched as if to embrace her sister. "Let go of the pain, Cordelia," she whispered, her voice steady and unwavering. "Come back to me. We can finally be at peace."

Nan's theatrical voice filled the room as she called out to her companions, "My dear friends, let us combine our love and light to defeat this dreadful revenant!" Mabel, a Cheshire-cat grin on her face, began to hum a cheery tune. Nan looked at her in confusion. "Is that— are you humming a song by The Village People?"

Without hesitation, Mabel threw her hands in the air and formed a letter Y with her body while swaying her hips back and forth. "Come join me, dear. It's the highest vibration tune I know." The two women continued to hum and dance along to 'YMCA', feeling their energy increase with each movement.

Bumbles, his tiny form vibrating with excitement, buzzed encouragingly. "Sweet nectar of kindness, melt away the shadows!" he chirped, leading the pixies in a shimmering dance around Cordelia.

As they focused their collective goodwill, a warm golden light began to emanate from their circle. Joy and happiness coursed through Nan, reminiscent of the fizz from a particularly spirited glass of Champagne. She slowed her movements and grasped Mabel's hand.

The golden light intensified, piercing Cordelia's spectral form. She let out a haunting wail, her figure contorting as the revenant's hold began to weaken.

"Cordelia," Bithia's voice rang out, clear and loving. "Let go of the pain, sister. Come back to me."

Cordelia's hollow, malevolent gaze flickered, her spectral form trembling like a candle caught in a tempest. The shadows that clung to her shimmered and fractured, her ethereal face contorted with pain and longing. "Bithia?" she whispered, her voice cracking with raw emotion. "I... I'm so sorry."

Her translucent figure began to shift, the edges softening as though a veil of darkness was being lifted. The oppressive shadow of the revenant unraveled from her form like smoke spiraling into the wind.

The revenant ripped free, its dark, writhing mass hissing and snarling as it twisted violently in the air.

Nan stumbled back, clutching the key around her neck. "Mabel, now!" she cried, her voice cutting through the chaos with the urgency of a crack of thunder. "The coffee tin! This is our chance!"

Mabel, her face crimson from exertion, curls disheveled and flower crown askew, lunged forward, the battered coffee tin clutched tightly in her hands. "Right-o, you nasty bit of ectoplasm!" she declared, her voice both fiery and unyieldingly cheerful. "Time for you to be grounded!"

The revenant hissed, its dark tendrils lashing out, but it recoiled as Bumbles and the pixies swarmed around it. Their luminous forms darted like fireflies, weaving nets of shimmering light that corralled the shadow.

"Push it toward the tin!" Nan shouted, her heart pounding as the pixies herded the howling entity. The revenant's resistance faltered under their combined effort, its form shrinking and writhing as it teetered on the edge of the tin's gaping mouth.

With a ferocious snarl the shadow plunged forward, and Mabel slammed the lid shut with a resounding clang. The tin rattled in her hands, a faint keening sound emanating from within as the revenant clawed uselessly at its prison.

Nan and Mabel exchanged a look, their breaths ragged, before moving in unison. With ceremonial care they placed their lavender-and-sage crowns atop the tin, the fragrant leaves humming with Gaia's energy.

"That should hold it," Nan murmured, her voice shaking as she straightened her dress, trying to gather herself. She stepped back, surveying their makeshift seal. "It's not every day one traps a revenant in a coffee tin after dancing to 'YMCA'."

"Well," Mabel said, "that was certainly more exciting than our usual afternoon tea. Perhaps you should consider installing a disco ball in the parlor."

Nan laughed. "That would be quite the surprise for Mossy!"

As the last echoes of the revenant's wail faded, a profound silence settled over the parlor. Cordelia's spirit, now free from the malevolent influence, shimmered with a soft, pearlescent light. Her once-hollow eyes now brimmed with tears as she gazed at her sister.

"Oh, Bithia," Cordelia whispered, her voice trembling with emotion. "Can you ever forgive me?"

Bithia floated towards her sister, her ethereal form radiating warmth. "My dear Cordelia, there's nothing to forgive. It was my own carelessness that led to the revenant being summoned during our séance." She paused. "But now, seeing you restored to your true self, my heart is filled with joy."

Nan watched the spectral reunion with misty eyes, her heart swelling with elation. She clasped Mabel's hand, squeezing it gently.

"I do believe we've witnessed a miracle, Mabel. A true miracle," Nan murmured, her voice thick with emotion.

Mabel nodded, dabbing at her eyes with a floral handkerchief. "Indeed we have, Nan. Though I must say, I never expected my first ghostly encounter to involve such a dramatic family reunion!"

The sisters turned to face their new friends, their forms now intertwined in a loving embrace.

"We cannot thank you enough." Bithia said, her refined accent tinged with gratitude. "You've freed us both from a terrible curse."

Cordelia nodded, a mischievous glint appearing in her eyes. "And now, if you'll permit us, we'd be delighted to haunt your charming establishment in a far more... agreeable manner."

Nan chuckled as she shook her head in amusement. "Well,

I suppose every respectable bed and breakfast ought to have a ghost or two. Though I must insist you refrain from rattling chains during teatime. Oh, and I insist that Mossy's beauty sleep be undisturbed."

As laughter filled the room, Nan felt a gentle tug on her dress. She looked down to see Bumbles gesturing urgently towards the coffee tin.

"Ah, yes," Nan said, her expression turning serious. "We have one last task to attend to, my friends."

The group made their way to the front garden, the coffee tin held carefully between Nan and Mabel. The sun cast a warm glow over the vibrant roses that lined the white picket fence.

"Here seems a fitting spot," Mabel declared, gesturing to a patch of earth near the front gate. "The roses will keep watch, and their thorns will discourage any meddling."

As Nan and Mabel began to dig the pixies flitted about, sprinkling the earth with a shimmering dust.

"What on earth are they doing?" Nan wondered aloud, pausing in her digging.

Mabel grinned, her eyes alight with wonder.

"It's the work of pixie magic, my dear. They're helping us with a little bit of faerie mischief to strengthen our efforts. If that revenant ever attempts to escape, it won't stand a chance against the power of the Fae!"

Once the hole was deep enough, they gently placed the coffee tin inside. The pixies then brought forth the crystals— hoplite, tourmaline, and agate—arranging them in a protective circle around the buried tin.

As they finished covering the makeshift grave with earth, Nan glanced up at the parlor window. Bithia and Cordelia stood there arm in arm, watching the proceedings with great interest.

Wiping her brow, Nan turned to her assembled friends—human and pixie alike. "Well, my dears," she said, her voice warm, "I do believe it's high time for a spot of tea. After all, vanquishing revenants is thirsty work!"

Mabel laughed. "I second that!"

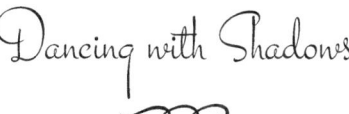 Dancing with Shadows

The deep ruby wine in their crystal goblets glinted like liquid jewels, while the haunting strains of "The Phantom of the Opera" wove a melody through the intimate space. Nan smiled, watching Mossy's agile fingers dance along the rim of his glass, his eyes closed in theatrical rapture.

"My dear," he intoned, his voice taking on a melodramatic flair he reserved for quoting his beloved musicals, "the wine you've chosen is a feast for the senses. One might say it's... 'the music of the night.'"

Nan chuckled, cutting into her perfectly roasted duck. "I'm delighted you approve, darling. San Sebastian's reserve Petite Sirah does pair wonderfully with my culinary efforts, doesn't it?"

Mossy nodded enthusiastically, his hair falling into his eyes as he leaned forward. "Indeed! One must embrace the local fare, after all. This sumptuous libation, with its notes of blackberry and vanilla, complements your duck and carrots exquisitely."

As they savored their meal, Mossy's eyes shone with excitement behind his thin spectacles. "Nan, my love, you'll never believe the adventure I had at the farmer's market today!"

Nan leaned in, captivated by her husband's childlike enthusiasm. "Do tell, Mossy. I'm all ears."

"Oh, Nan, it was positively enchanting!" Mossy exclaimed, gesturing grandly with his fork. "The produce gleamed like gemstones, the vendors were as cheerful as Shakespearean jesters, and the entire market felt like stepping into a Wordsworth poem brought to life. Truly, a feast for the senses!"

Nan smiled indulgently, thinking how even a simple trip to the market became a poetic odyssey in Mossy's mind.

"But the true highlight," he continued, pausing dramatically, "was an encounter with a gentleman named Rufus. We struck up the most fascinating conversation about... are you ready for this, Nan? Pickleball!"

"Pickleball?" Nan repeated, her eyebrows rising in amusement. "My dear Mossy, I never took you for an athlete."

Mossy chuckled, a faint blush coloring his cheeks. "Nor did I, my love. But Rufus spoke of it with such passion! He's invited me to play at Pictona. Can you imagine? Your dreamy poet of a husband, wielding a paddle on the court?"

As Mossy continued to regale her with tales of his market adventures, Nan felt a warmth spreading through her chest that had nothing to do with the wine. She pondered at how, even after all these years, Mossy could still surprise her with his whimsical enthusiasm for life's little joys.

"Perhaps," Nan speculated, raising her glass in a toast, "this pickleball endeavor will inspire a new collection of sports-themed poetry, my dear?"

Mossy's eyes gleamed as he clinked his glass against hers. "Ah, Nan," he sighed dramatically, once again channeling the Phantom, "you alone can make my song take flight!"

Nan's laughter tinkled like wind chimes, a melodious

counterpoint to the haunting strains of 'The Music of the Night' playing softly in the background. "Oh, Mossy," she teased, her voice rich with affection, "I can just picture you now, resplendent in your athletic wear. You'll be the talk of Pictona, my dear—a veritable Byron of the pickleball court!"

As Nan spoke her gaze drifted to the window, where a flicker of movement caught her eye. There, pressed against the glass, were tiny, luminous faces. It was the pixies, drawn by the lively conversation and warm atmosphere within. She stifled a smile, careful not to alert Mossy to their presence.

Oblivious to their diminutive audience, Mossy's face lit up with boyish excitement. "Can you believe it, Nan? Embarking on a new sporting adventure at my age? It's positively invigorating!"

He paused, taking a sip of wine before continuing, his voice softening. "You know, my dear, it's not just the game itself that appeals to me. It's the sense of community, the camaraderie. Rufus spoke of friendships forged over friendly matches, of laughter shared between serves."

Nan reached across the table, clasping Mossy's hand in hers. "Oh, my darling," she said warmly, "I'm so pleased. You know how I worry about you spending too much time lost in your books and verses."

Mossy's eyes misted slightly as he squeezed Nan's hand. "Indeed, my love. Perhaps it's time for this old poet to step out from behind his quill and parchment, to write a new chapter filled with... what did Rufus call them? Ah yes, 'dinks' and 'volleys'."

"Speaking of thrilling new chapters," Nan began, a mischievous twinkle in her eye as she leaned across the table. "I have some rather extraordinary news to share." She paused dramatically, savoring the suspense. "Our spectral squatter is gone! Banished, exorcised, and sent packing!" Mossy's eyebrows shot up, his fork clattering against his plate. "Good heavens, Nan! Your plan worked? You mean to say you've banished the revenant?"

Nan nodded, a triumphant smile playing across her lips. "Indeed we have, my love, with quite a bit of help from the pixies. It was quite the spectacle, I must say." She recounted the encounter with vivid detail, her hands dancing through the air as she spoke.

Mossy listened, enraptured, his dinner forgotten.

"Oh, Mossy, it was extraordinary!" Nan's eyes shone with excitement.

Mossy reached across the table, clasping Nan's hands in his. "My brave, brilliant Nannette," he said, his voice thick with emotion. "I couldn't be prouder if I tried. To think, I'm married to a genuine spirit-banishing heroine!"

Nan blushed prettily, squeezing Mossy's hands. "Oh hush, you old charmer. But I must admit it does feel rather wonderful to have triumphed. And now, my love, we can finally move forward with our plans for the B&B!"

"Indeed, we can!" Mossy exclaimed, his face alight with joy. "Just imagine it, Nan—our home filled with guests, sharing in the magic and mystery of this place. Why, we'll be the gem of Daytona Beach!"

As they sat there, hands entwined across the table, Nan felt a surge of love for her dear Mossy.

Nan raised her crystal goblet, the candlelight dancing off the deep ruby liquid within. "A toast, my darling Mossy," she declared, her voice carrying the lyrical quality of a bygone era. "To shared victories, new friendships and pursuits, and the delightful future that awaits!"

Mossy beamed as the golden glow of the candles reflected off his own raised glass. "To us, my dear," he replied, his voice serene. "May our days be filled with wonder, and our nights with... well, perhaps a touch less of the supernatural, if you please."

They clinked their glasses together, the crystal singing a delicate melody. As they sipped the rich Petite Sirah, savoring its notes of blackberry and spice, Mossy hummed contentedly. "Ah, 'Music of the Night' indeed," he mused, referencing their background ambiance.

The air in the dining room shifted, a subtle chill weaving through the candlelit warmth. Mossy's eyes widened as the faint outlines of two figures emerged, solidifying into shimmering forms. Bithia, draped in tasteful Victorian finery, exuded an aura of serene authority, while Cordelia's lace gown seemed to ripple as if caught in an unseen breeze.

His scholarly demeanor momentarily shaken, Mossy found himself quoting breathlessly, "'In sleep he sang to me, in dreams he came...'" He blinked rapidly, his mind racing to reconcile the supernatural sight before him. "Good heavens, Nan," he whispered.

As 'Angel of Music' soared through the room Mossy's eyes widened to saucers, his spectacles sliding precariously down his nose. The spirits before him shimmered in the candlelight, their otherworldly forms mesmerizing.

"My word," he whispered, his voice trembling with awe as if he were gazing upon a painting come to life. "Magnificent... absolutely magnificent." He blinked, then added, "Nan, do you suppose they'd stay for dessert? Or perhaps a spirited debate on Tennyson?"

His eyes darted between Bithia and Cordelia, drinking in every ethereal detail. "Nan, my dear, do you see them as well?"

But as the music reached its climax Mossy's face paled, his cheeks draining of color. He swayed in his seat, his fingers gripping the edge of the table. "I... I feel rather faint," he murmured, his poetic eloquence deserting him.

Nan rose gracefully, the hem of her sundress brushing the polished floor as she crossed to Mossy's side. "Mossy, darling," she soothed, her hand resting lightly on his shoulder. "Deep breaths now. They're harmless—mostly." Her warm smile carried just a hint of amusement.

Mossy leaned into Nan's embrace, his dampened forehead brushing against her powdered cheek. "To see them," he whispered, his voice filled with awe. "To actually see them, Nan. It's... it's beyond anything I could have imagined."

He trembled as he slowly extended his hand towards the ghostly figures. The air around him seemed to thicken, charged with an energy that caused every hair on his body to stand on end. He hesitated, his hand suspended in midair, caught between fascination and trepidation.

"I say, Nan," he whispered, his voice quavering like a violin string, "do you suppose they might... well, that is to say... can one actually touch a spirit?"

Nan's warm chuckle tickled his ear. "Oh, Mossy dear, I wouldn't recommend it. They're rather particular about personal space, you know."

Bithia's luminous form glided forward, her every movement as fluid as a moonbeam on water. With an artistic flourish she reached for Nan's wine glass, lifting it in a silent toast. The crystal refracted the candlelight, scattering rainbows across the table.

Mossy's breath caught in his throat. "Good heavens," he murmured, "she's positively radiant."

Cordelia, not to be outdone, drifted towards the nearest candle. Her hollow eyes gleamed as she bent forward, her spectral lips pursed. With a gentle puff she extinguished the flame, plunging that corner of the room into shadow.

"Oh my," Mossy gasped, his grip on Nan's hand tightening.

As quickly as they had appeared both spirits vanished, leaving behind only a lingering chill in the air and the faintest scent of jasmine.

Nan patted Mossy's hand reassuringly. "There, there,

darling. It's all in good fun, nothing to worry about. They're just saying hello in their own special way."

Mossy furrowed his brow, his scholarly mind racing to make sense of what he'd just witnessed. "But Nan, how can you be so calm about this? We've just had dinner with the dead!"

Silence fell over the dining room, broken only by the soft ticking of the grandfather clock in the corner. Mossy sat motionless, his eyes wide and unfocused, as if trying to replay the spectral visitation in his mind.

Nan rose gracefully from her seat. "I believe this calls for something a tad stronger than wine, my dear," she said, her voice betraying her amusement. She glided to the antique sideboard, her heels clicking softly against the polished floorboards.

Returning with a crystal tumbler, she placed it before Mossy. "Here, darling, for your nerves. A touch of liquid courage, as they say."

Mossy's long, graceful fingers curled around the glass. "Thank you, my love," he murmured, bringing the amber liquid to his lips. He took a sip, savoring the smoky flavor. "Ah, that does hit the spot. Rather like a poet's muse in liquid form, wouldn't you say?"

Nan chuckled, settling back into her chair. "Only you could find poetry in a moment of supernatural shock, Mossy dear."

As the warmth of the scotch spread through him, Mossy's gaze drifted to the window. His eyes widened with wonder. "I say, Nan. Your garden has attracted quite a lot of fireflies. How utterly enchanting."

Nan followed his gaze, a knowing smile playing on her lips. The 'fireflies' danced and swirled in patterns too intricate to be natural, their light a touch too ethereal.

"Yes, quite... enchanting," Nan echoed, her lips curving in

a knowing smile. She reached for her goblet, letting the moment linger before adding brightly, "So, Mossy, tell me more about this Pickleball revolution. Will your paddle be inscribed with 'To dink, perchance to volley'? Or shall we keep it simpler: 'Full paddle jacket'?"

From Ghosts to Guests

The golden rays of morning sunlight danced across the kitchen table, casting a warm glow on the stack of waffles steaming between Nan and Mossy. Nan stifled a laugh as Mossy tugged at his neon green pickleball shoes, their brightness clashing with the dignified air he usually reserved for tweed and leather loafers. "I feel like a court jester, my dear," he muttered, smoothing the collar of his crisp white polo. "Do you suppose this garish attire is absolutely necessary for the sport?"

"You look smashing, darling. Positively smashing," Nan cooed.

Mossy grinned and puffed out his chest. "Did you know that in pickleball, the serve must be made underhand and below the waist?"

Nan nodded as she spread jam on her waffle. "Fascinating, darling. And how does one score in this curious sport?"

As Mossy launched into a detailed explanation of pickleball scoring, Nan's mind wandered to her own plans for the day. The thought of cruising along the beach with Mabel, the salty breeze in her hair, filled her with excitement.

"Oh, Mossy," she interrupted, "you'll do splendidly. Now, what do you think of my new ensemble?" She stood, twirling in her skort and sleeveless sweater.

Mossy's eyes widened behind his spectacles. "My dear, you look positively radiant. Like a sun-kissed nymph ready to frolic by the sea."

Nan laughed, a tinkling sound that seemed to brighten the room. "You silver-tongued devil. Now help me pack this picnic basket, won't you?"

She tilted her head, a playful grin lighting her face. "What a curious day we've planned: you, dueling with tiny paddles in neon glory, and I, pedaling the sands of Daytona with Mabel. Quite the picture, isn't it?"

Mossy nodded, a dreamy look crossing his face. "Indeed. Life is full of unexpected joys, my love. Speaking of which..." He trailed off, a mischievous glint in his eye.

"Mr. Nettles, what are you up to?"

He grinned, taking her hand. "I have a surprise for you, my dear. Come along."

As they ascended the stairs, Nan's heart fluttered. What could her darling husband have in store?

When they reached the attic door, Mossy paused with a flourish, his spectacles catching the morning light. "Close your eyes, my dear, and prepare yourself for wonder."

Nan obliged, her pulse quickening. The creak of the door opening was followed by Mossy's soft footsteps guiding her forward.

"Now, my love," he murmured, his voice tinged with delight, "behold."

Nan opened her eyes and gasped, her hands flying to her mouth. The attic had been transformed into a writer's haven: an antique desk polished to a golden sheen stood atop a hand-woven Turkish rug, the skylight spilling sunlight onto walls lined with books. A cozy reading nook in the corner beckoned, complete with plump cushions and a knitted throw.

"Oh, Mossy," she breathed, turning slowly to take in the floor-to-ceiling bookshelves, the cozy reading nook, and the skylights that framed puffy white clouds. "It's... it's perfect."

Mossy watched her, beaming with pride. "Do you truly like it, my dear?"

Nan turned to him, her eyes shining. "Like it? Mossy, I adore it. It's as if you've plucked a dream from my mind and made it real."

As they embraced, Nan felt a wave of gratitude wash over her. For her loving husband, for their charming B&B, and for the magical life they were building together.

As Nan's fingers trailed along the smooth surface of the antique desk, a shimmer in the corner caught her eye. There, partially hidden behind a bookshelf, stood Bithia and Cordelia, their ethereal forms flickering like candlelight. Nan's heart leapt with delight but she quickly composed herself, offering the spectral sisters a subtle wink.

"My stars, Nan," Bithia's melodious voice floated into her thoughts. "This is sheer perfection! A writing room fit for the finest novels. Shall we assist with crafting a tale of great intrigue and romance?"

Cordelia, her features softened by curiosity, added, "Indeed. Perhaps a tale of sisterly reconciliation... with a dash of haunting, of course."

Nan suppressed a chuckle, turning back to Mossy. "Darling, your thoughtfulness overwhelms me. But, as it happens, I have a surprise of my own to share."

Mossy's eyebrows rose with curiosity. "Oh? Do tell, my dear."

Nan clasped her hands together, barely containing her excitement. "We've received our first booking! A lovely couple wishes to stay for a week with their extended family, and—"

she paused for dramatic effect, "—they want to hold their wedding here at our B&B!"

Mossy's face lit up like a child on Christmas morning. "Splendid news, my love! Our first guests, and a wedding to boot!"

"Oh, Mossy, I can hardly contain myself," Nan gushed, her mind already whirling with plans. "I'm envisioning a three-tiered Victoria sponge, adorned with fresh strawberries and edible flowers from Mabel's garden. And for the reception, I'll prepare my famous lobster bisque, roast duck with cherry sauce, and..."

As Nan rattled off her culinary plans she caught sight of Bithia and Cordelia, now hovering near the skylights. The ghostly sisters exchanged a look of amused exasperation, no doubt wondering how they'd manage to assist with Nan's writing when she'd be knee-deep in wedding preparations.

What a delightful predicament, Nan thought, her heart full of joy. *A new writing room, spectral muses, and a wedding to plan. How wonderfully, perfectly mad!*

Mossy grasped Nan's hands in his own. "My darling, you've outdone yourself once again. This is positively marvelous!" He cleared his throat, adopting a theatrical pose. "As the Bard himself once wrote, 'Love is not love which alters when it alteration finds, or bends with the remover to remove.'"

Nan chortled, her cheeks flushing with warmth. "Oh, Mossy, trust you to find the perfect sonnet for the occasion."

"But wait, there's more!" Mossy exclaimed, his excitement building. "For what is a wedding without a touch of Browning? 'Grow old along with me! The best is yet to be, the last of life, for which the first was made.'"

As Mossy continued his poetic serenade, Nan's mind began to race with all the preparations they needed to make. She gently squeezed Mossy's hands, interrupting his recitation.

"Darling, as much as I adore your impromptu poetry-reciting, we mustn't dawdle. There's so much to do before our guests arrive!"

Her gaze darted around the attic, mentally cataloging their tasks. "We'll need to give the guest rooms a final once-over, prepare welcome baskets... Oh, and we simply must stock up on groceries. I'm thinking fresh lavender sachets for the pillows, and perhaps some locally made saltwater taffy for their baskets."

Mossy nodded eagerly, already reaching for a notepad. "Indeed, my love. Shall I make a list? We wouldn't want to forget a single detail in our quest for innkeeping perfection."

He scribbled furiously on the notepad. "My dear, allow me to shoulder the burden of these practical matters," he declared with a flourish of his pen. "I shall contact our esteemed guests forthwith to confirm their arrival time. And fear not, for I shall ensure our humble abode is stocked with every conceivable essential."

"Oh, Mossy, you're a treasure. What would I do without you?"

As Mossy began to recite an impromptu ode to his organizational skills, Nan's attention was drawn to the ethereal forms of Bithia and Cordelia. The spectral sisters were practically vibrating with excitement, their Victorian gowns shimmering like gossamer in the attic's soft light.

Bithia floated closer to Nan. "A wedding at Nettles' B&B! How utterly enchanting, Nan. I daresay this calls for a touch of spectral elegance. Perhaps a reading of Victorian poetry to bless the union?"

Cordelia grinned, her usual sharpness softened by excitement. "Or perhaps a subtle haunting during the vows? Nothing too dramatic, just a flicker of candlelight to set the mood."

Nan suppressed a giggle, imagining the guests' reactions to

a ghostly duet. She whispered under her breath, "Let's keep the supernatural surprises to a minimum, shall we? We want to charm our guests, not terrify them."

Mossy drifted towards the attic window, his gaze drawn to the verdant expanse below. "Nan, my darling, come see this," he called softly, his voice imbued with wonder. Nan joined him, peering over his shoulder at the vibrant garden below. Sunlight filtered through the canopy of ancient oaks, dappling the velvet lawn with golden patches. Roses in full bloom spilled over their trellises, their colors a palette of crimson, blush, and gold. Among the blossoms pixies flitted like living jewels, their gossamer wings trailing sparkles that shimmered in the gentle breeze.

"Isn't it marvelous?" Mossy sighed, oblivious to the magical display. "The way the light plays on the petals..."

Nan smiled, squeezing his hand. "It's perfect, love."

Mossy's eyes widened. "By Jove, I've had an epiphany! We shall hold the wedding outside, in this very garden!"

"What a splendid idea," Nan replied, her heart swelling with joy. She imagined the pixies, unseen by the guests, adding their own enchantment to the ceremony.

As they descended the stairs, Nan's mind whirled with possibilities. She gathered her picnic basket, its wicker sides cool against her fingers.

At the front door Mossy pulled her close, planting a tender kiss on her lips. "You look absolutely radiant, my dear," he murmured. "Like Aurora herself, ready to cycle forth and greet the day."

Nan chuckled, mounting her cruiser bicycle. "Oh, Mossy, you silver-tongued charmer."

He raised a hand dramatically, reciting:

"Pedal forth, my love, on spoked steed so bright,
Your beauty outshines the morning's fair light.
May your journey be swift, your picnic sublime,

And know that my heart follows you through time."

Nan stood at the garden gate, watching Mossy's car disappear around the bend, her heart light and buoyant. The gentle hum of his engine faded into the stillness of the morning, leaving behind the cheerful trill of songbirds and the soft murmur of the fountain. She turned back to the house, its freshly painted exterior glowing in the sunlight. The intricate gingerbread trim seemed to wink at her conspiratorially, as though sharing a secret only the house could know.

Her gaze drifted upward to the attic window, where she spotted Bithia and Cordelia, their ghostly forms shimmering faintly. They waved with enthusiasm, their translucent smiles brimming with approval. Nan pressed the cool metal of the house key against her chest, feeling its reassuring touch—a symbol of responsibility, resilience, and the bond she now shared with the home and its spectral occupants.

In the garden Bumbles and a flurry of pixies danced among the blooms, their tiny, glowing forms sparkling like morning dew kissed by the sun. Their playful magic sent ripples of energy through the flowers, making the petals tremble as if alive with joy.

Nan mounted her bicycle, inhaling deeply as a wave of gratitude washed over her. The house, once a shadow of its former glory, now stood proud and alive, a haven for both the living and the spectral. Bithia and Cordelia's reconciliation had banished the lingering tension, their presence now a source of warmth instead of unrest. And Mabel, with her flower lore and kind heart, had become a steadfast friend—as natural a fit in Nan's life as the blooms in her garden.

With one last look at the pixie-kissed roses and a discreet nod to her spectral companions, Nan pushed off on her bicycle. The salty breeze brushed at her curls as she pedaled down the path to meet Mabel for their beachside adventure.

"Life," she murmured, resting a hand over the key that hung at her chest, "is truly brimming with magic."

About the Author

Chrissy Chicory is a Florida author known for her enchanting blend of magic, mystery, and heartfelt storytelling. Her work spans multiple genres, including magical realism, cozy mysteries, and personal development, all infused with whimsy and warmth.

In the **Culebra Chronicles**, Chrissy brings the historic streets of St. Augustine, Florida, to life with a mix of magical realism and thrilling intrigue. The series follows courageous characters unraveling ancient mysteries where history and magic intertwine.

The **Nettles B&B Paracozy Series** showcases her flair for blending cozy mystery with supernatural charm. Set in a quirky bed-and-breakfast in Daytona Beach, the series follows the eccentric Nan and Mossy Nettles as they navigate ghostly shenanigans, mischievous pixies, and small-town secrets. With humor and heart, these stories offer the perfect escape for fans of whimsical mysteries.

Beyond fiction, Chrissy's **Ink and Verse** series celebrates the art of handwriting through classical poetry. Designed for teens and adults, these workbooks combine cursive practice with literary masterpieces, inspiring creativity while preserving the beauty of the written word.

Her **Lucid Living Series** explores mindful growth and intentional living. This personal development collection encourages readers to embrace awareness, intuition, and purposeful action, providing tools to cultivate resilience and self-compassion.

Chrissy's books offer a comforting escape—like a warm cup of tea on a rainy day or a moonlit stroll through a secret garden. Whether unraveling supernatural mysteries, preserving the tradition of cursive writing, or guiding readers toward a more mindful life, her work invites curiosity, creativity, and transformation.

With each new release, Chrissy Chicory continues to captivate and inspire, making her a beloved voice in contemporary fiction and personal development.

To keep up with all things **Chrissy Chicory**, including new releases, behind-the-scenes updates, and exclusive content, be sure to sign up for her newsletter. Visit **ChrissyChicory.com** to explore her books and join the adventure!

www.ingramcontent.com/pod-product-compliance
Lightning Source LLC
Chambersburg PA
CBHW060352180626
46817CB00008B/2981